Eternal Wanderings

The Continuing Journey of Kara O'Keefe

Danielle Ackley-McPhail

PAPER PHOENIX PRESS

Pennsville, NJ

PUBLISHED BY
Paper Phoenix Press
A division of eSpec Books
PO Box 242
Pennsville, NJ 08070
www.especbooks.com

ISBN: 978-1-942990-02-4
ISBN (ebook): 978-1-942990-06-2

Interior Design: Danielle McPhail
Sidhe na Daire
www.sidhenadaire.com

Art credits from http://www.shutterstock.com
Interior Art: vector musical composition ©BuketGvozdey
Cover Images:
Road in magic dark forest © Elena Schweitzer
A musician playing outdoors, a violin © yuda chen

Cover Design: Mike McPhail, McP Digital Graphics
Copyediting: Greg Schauer

Based on the Eternal Cycle Trilogy of Novels
by Danielle Ackley-McPhail

Yesterday's Dreams
Tomorrow's Memories
Today's Promise

Never wander aimlessly,
but to a purpose.

For all of those like me
whose only children live and laugh
within the pages of a book and
the landscape of a reader's mind

Contents

Chapter One

As Kara O'Keefe followed Sveta through the portal leaving *Tir na nÓg* she staggered and nearly fell to her knees. At the heart of the Land of Youth, in Goibhniu's court of *Mór Halla*, she had not grasped the scope of the change the Naming had wrought in her, but upon crossing into the mortal world it became clear. In joining the pattern of her life to the Great Wall, she had also connected her soul to the race of *Tuatha de Danaan*. She had known this but had not felt the impact earlier, deep as she had been in their magical realm. Beyond those bounds, she felt the links like silken threads trailing back to each and every one of her new kin. Not restricting, just connecting.

To think months ago she'd been nothing more than a simple, if gifted, music teacher from Queens, New York, struggling to save the house she'd grown up in. About as far as one could get from joining the magical ranks of immortal elves.

It was one thing to know she bore a *Sidhe* soul, their second-most cherished one at that, but to feel the connection to her people...to know to her very core where they were, in rough direction and distance, if not precise location...the awe nearly overwhelmed her.

She drew a sharp breath and resisted the impulse to examine those threads more closely, in search of one in particular.

Sveta looked back at Kara's gasp, concern and confusion mingled in her gaze.

"It's okay," Kara murmured. "I just stumbled.

"Thank you for waiting for me," she added.

Sveta nodded but said nothing, clearly anxious to be away. Kara followed the young woman down the path leading to the Romani camp, fascinated by the long fall of her blue-black hair and the swish of her full skirt. As beautiful as it was with its bright colors and bold patterns, Kara couldn't imagine wearing such a thing in the day-to-day. But this wasn't New York or even Dublin. Things would be different among the Rom. Kara did not have the first clue just *how* different.

A little nervous, she reached up and fingered the rune-engraved copper pendant hanging from its leather lanyard around her neck. She wore it in memory of Granddame Rose, a reminder of both her promise and Rose's sacrifice. The case containing Kara's violin, Quicksilver, lay comfortingly across her back and the sprite, Beag Scath, had settled down to cuddle beneath the curtain of her hair. The rest of her scant things had already been taken to the caravan.

It felt odd to leave her parents behind. In many ways, she loathed to leave them or *Tir na nÓg*, but, even if not for her vow to Granddame Rose, leaving was the prudent thing to do. Everyone needed time to come to terms with this reordering of their reality—herself included.

Though born mostly human, Kara O'Keefe possessed a *Sidhe* soul. And not just any soul, but that of Anu, twin to the goddess Danu, from whom all other *Sidhe* had been reborn. It was difficult to come to grips with that, particularly when in the midst of the *Tuatha de Danaan*—the Children of Danu—not all of whom were pleased to welcome her as one of their own, despite evidence they could not refute.

After the Battle of the Knock—where the demigods Olcas and Dubh attempted to besiege the gates of *Tir na nÓg*—Granddame Rose had offered Kara a place with the Kalderaš Clan, an offer seconded by the rest of the clan on the night Kara had first played for them. Astounding, really, given the insular nature of the culture. Accepting that place now seemed the best way to distance herself, as well as to fulfill the vow she had made.

Rose's grandson, Tony DeLocosta, had been possessed by Olcas. At the same time as Rose had offered Kara shelter with the Rom, she had also made her vow to free Tony. Physically, Kara already had when she defeated the demigods, but Tony's soul remained in torment at the memory of the atrocities committed using his body, including the murder of his grandmother by his own hand, if not his will.

The Rom had already collected Rose's remains...and her grandson. Kara had the sense that none of the clan were too happy about *that*, but the Rom took care of their own. That was one of the first things Rose had ever said to her: *Family before all others.*

The Rom clearly weren't too comfortable about honoring their offer to Kara, either, but hadn't denied her. She wouldn't have blamed them if they had, given the turmoil that seemed to follow her. First in New York, then again in *Tir na nÓg*. She never invited it, but it came just the same.

As they approached the caravan, Kara was puzzled by the faint haze and scent of acrid smoke on the air. She reached out and gripped Sveta's shoulder. "What's going on? I thought we were leaving..."

The woman flinched and her gaze shrouded further as she turned to look back, her eyes darting to view the far side of the clearing. Kara spied a fresh cairn just this side of the tree line, and beside it, Granddame Rose's traditional wagon, or vardo, engulfed in flame. One of the *Sidhe* stood beside it, containing the sparks and embers with a mage shield.

Kara's brow dipped down and her grip on Sveta's shoulder tightened. "What's going on here...and *where* is Tony?"

"*Dinlo gorgio*," —*stupid outsider*, Sveta muttered beneath her breath as she spat on the ground, her tone sharp and her expression offended. "That one is already tucked in his wagon, ready to leave. As *we* should be..." She looked like she might say more, but Markos, leader of the Kalderaš Clan, called out harshly in Romani from the head of the caravan. At the sound of his voice, Sveta shrugged Kara's hand from her shoulder and continued on.

"Now is not the time," she muttered. "We must be away before night falls."

Frowning, Kara glanced back at the burning vardo. She waved farewell to the *Sidhe* guarding the flames then followed, climbing into the wagon Sveta indicated. Kara still felt the leader of the Rom scowling back at them from the seat of his vardo. Inside Sveta's wagon, three young boys stared at Kara from the built-in bunks lining the walls. She jumped as the door closed sharply behind her, but the boys did not laugh or even giggle. They continued to watch her with dark, solemn eyes as the wagon lurched and began to move. Grimacing, Kara braced herself against the wall before moving to sit at a bench inside the wagon.

She wondered if claiming a place with the Kalderaš Clan had been wise after all.

The urge to howl gripped her. The need to turn back and fight shook her, but the fleeing one resisted. In their kind, the instinct for survival ran stronger than any other impulse. She broke the bond of her pack to preserve her kind through the young within her. As rarely happened in their long existence, one of the *Bás* fled lest their race meet its end. Slinking through the brush, she dropped her jaw and drew hard on the air. She tasted nothing of those who hunted her, nothing of choice prey, but something tinged the air temptingly close. Huffing slightly, she crept forward, parting the brush to peer out. A corporeal creature knelt in the clearing, arranging sticks in a peculiar manner before kindling a flame and settling into a sack upon the ground. The *Bás* narrowed her gaze and watched. This one was a pale shadow of their chosen prey. No power well. No essence. Just a hint of energy not worth the effort to claim, and most certainly not sufficient for nesting the *Bás*'s young. Still, the creature drew her. Tickled the memory of the Black One and how he had hidden his spirit within another like a whelp returning to the nest. The *Bás* were mostly creatures of spirit, not earth. Could she hide in such a manner? Such a concept filled her mouth with a foul, bitter taste, but the need to survive gripped her harder and shoved. The *Bás* dropped low and slinked forward. Muscles rippled in subtle waves, and a low trill sounded deep in her throat, unbidden. The *Bás* stilled and dropped her belly to the ground, but the not-prey did not bounce up or flee.

She watched and drew herself forward. Again, she sampled the air. This one had the faintest of flavors that spoke of shared blood with the *Daoine Maithé*—in their own tongue, the Good People. To the *Bás* they were the cursed ones; just as to the cursed ones, the *Bás* were the *Namhaid*—or enemy.

The not-prey likewise had no sense of self-preservation, unaware that death stalked nearby. The *Bás* crept closer yet. Close enough to touch. She ran light fingers over soft, weak flesh and rough coverings. She leaned forward for a closer sampling of scent. A gentle tugging came as spirit clung to spirit.

On impulse the *Bás* hissed and drew back into a crouch, razor-sharp teeth bared and claws extended. The creature slumbered on, faintly snoring, as if safe and secure in its own den. It took long moments for the *Bás* to calm. She moved about the clearing in a not-quite stalk, skin twitching beneath its pale, velvety pelt and eyes searching for other threats.

Slowly she settled, again squatting close to what had become now-prey, of sorts, for instinct now spoke to the *Bás* most insistently. Again, memories of the Black One rose. Might the *Bás* hide within, as he had? Reaching out, she laid a hand to the other's flesh, once more felt the tugging of their spirits as they twined. Following an impulse, she lay herself down upon the slumbering one, form aligned with form. The now-prey twitched as if deep in a dream. A moan flowed out on labored breath just tinged with fear. Limbs thrashed in jerking, uncoordinated motions. The *Bás*'s purr increased as the now-prey sought to free herself from the melding. *Too late,* the hunter murmured as she gripped that captured soul tight and sank deeper into the other's body. She savored the bite of her host's panic as they became one.

By the time they set camp late that night, Kara was too wiped out to do anything but sleep. When she woke the next morning in the wagon, Sveta and her sons were nowhere to be found.

The same with Beag Scath.

Trying not to worry what mischief the sprite might be up to, Kara helped herself to some oatmeal left warming on the wood-burning stove before slinging Quicksilver's case across her back and venturing out into the cool bright day. It felt like early spring or mid-fall. For all she knew, it could be either. She'd lost all track of time in the *Sidhe* realm. Drawing a deep breath, she basked in the warm sun and took joy in the bright blue sky, two things to never be taken for granted.

She wandered a while, among the wagons, some brightly painted and built from wood in the tradition of the Romani people, others battered metal caravans traveling under their own power or pulled behind trucks or cars, as you would find at any campground around the world. All of them bore the essence of the Rom, brightly painted, delightfully unique. Each family had set their own camp, with carpets on the ground and cushions for sitting. Some had fire pits, others had portable grills. At some of the hearths, awnings had been raised for shelter from the elements, at others, battery-powered faerie lights had been strung from poles but the space left open to the sky.

As she explored, Kara relaxed into the day, enjoying the real-world magic of the Romani culture, free and untethered from any society but their own. Both the exotic and the mundane mingled as they adapted what they came by for their uses. Kara watched one group of women weaving a rug of intricate geometric patterns out of rags, while another bundled and hung herbs to dry. Some of the men were making horseshoes at a makeshift forge surrounded by smoke and ash and dry heat. If not for their dark scowls, she would have watched them longer, but instead quickly moved along. The sound of their hammers striking steel rang through the camp blending with the women's chatter in an industrious song Kara longed to join.

Throughout the morning, she remained polite and cheerful, despite the lukewarm reception she received. Everyone seemed wary. Not hostile, but too reserved to be welcoming. Kara asked questions when something puzzled her, even offered to help when she saw them at their chores, but no one would speak to her in English—though she had no doubt the majority of them could—if they said anything at all. She gave up and continued exploring, wandering the camp that was, for now, her home, trying not to get in anyone's way. At one point, she felt eyes focus on her, more so than the wary curiosity she'd met all morning. Her shoulders tensed with the weight of that gaze. Casually looking around, she noticed Markos, the caravan leader, his arms crossed and expression unreadable as he watched her. Though the sun picked out threads of silver woven through the waves of his dark brown hair, she could not tell if age or strain had added the faint webbing of lines across his forehead and around his bright blue eyes.

She met his gaze with a faint smile and nodded respectfully.

Markos's brow dipped into a frown, clearly not happy she had noticed him. He dropped his arms and turned sharply away, heading across the camp to his wagon. Kara waited until he was out of sight then resumed her wandering.

The uncertainty she encountered from the adults apparently did not extend to the children. As Kara explored the camp the sound of muffled giggles and scampering feet followed her until she'd amassed a fair parade of young followers. A smile lifted her lips, and she began to skip and dance with joy at the curiosity of youth, which broke down the walls of reserve. She didn't look too closely, but she noticed a few adult eyes crinkle at the goings-on, even if their lips refused to smile.

The giggles grew louder. Her timid shadows pranced forward to join her as she continued to dance. As they neared the center clearing of the camp, she slowed and tried—though not too hard—to mimic their fluid moves as they twirled and leaped and clearly executed steps unique to the Rom. The children collapsed, their giggles blossoming into laughter at her comic efforts.

Breathing hard more for effect, than from the effort, Kara flopped to one of the rough logs set around the center clearing, where an unlit bonfire sat waiting for the evening. Remembering the night she'd played for these same Rom after the Battle of the Knock, Kara drew Quicksilver from her case and began to tune the violin. That quick, the laughing and horsing around died down. The children turned bright eyes upon her, as did no few of the adults. Drawing a deep, calm breath, Kara allowed a subtle smile to grace her lips, while inside she sang hallelujah. Music truly was the universal language. Not that she expected to be automatically accepted now, but this gave her hope.

Kara allowed herself to savor this moment of happiness and peace. As the children settled in a circle around her she began to play, not bothering with anyone else's composition but allowing Quicksilver's own voice to rise in an unchoreographed song.

As the notes filled the camp, Kara felt Danu's essence stir from where it resided in the violin and wrap around her in approval. Bolstered by the goddess, Kara continued to play through what was left of the morning until her fingers stung and her bow arm burned. The children came and went as they were presumably called to chores, but as the noon hour drew near they wandered back, followed by their parents. With delight, Kara noted that some carried instruments—fiddles and guitars and pan flutes and spoons, but also a darbuka, ukulele, cimbalom, bodhran, and half a dozen other instruments she wouldn't have known the names of if she hadn't studied at Julliard. Others carried food, or drink, or nothing but themselves. However they came, it brought a broad grin to Kara's face.

Not unsurprisingly, Beag Scath came with them, the shameless sprite winding about the ankles of those carrying food, his thatch of unruly curls—a mix of every shade of red, brown and gold—bobbing enthusiastically to the music. Most shocking was the fact that he wore his own form—human in feature and proportion, but about the size of a twelve-inch action figure— rather than the cat seeming he usually favored. Not until that moment had she realized she'd not seen one feline in the camp. She filed that thought away for later consideration and turned her gaze back on her little friend. Kara laughed as he scampered just out of reach of the squealing children, before circling back toward the food bearers. After all, this group of Rom were friend to the *Sidhe* and surely were familiar with faelings such as Beag Scath.

Kara smiled as she continued to play.

"You they can keep their distance from, easily," a woman spoke softly beside her, "the music, not at all. Smart that you should play. It reminds them you have done so before at our fire as an invited guest, and that they did not mind you so much then."

Kara jumped a little at the unexpected comment, but quickly relaxed. It was comforting to hear words in English after a day of nothing but what she expected were Romani curses. She turned to find Sveta at her side. The woman sat down beside her and held out a mug of some herbal tea. Kara's belly rumbled at the spicy scent mingled with the rich aroma coming from the foods being passed around.

"Thank you." Kara set Quicksilver down beside her as other musicians began to play and accepted Sveta's peace offering, for such it was.

After the impromptu lunch and concert, the members of the caravan rose and returned to their tasks. Some nodded at Kara as they passed, while the children waved or threw their arms around her in quick impulsive hugs. Beside her, Sveta laughed softly.

"Very smart indeed." The woman rose and waved for Kara to join her. "Come, Markos would like to talk to you."

Kara tensed for just a moment as she remembered the clan leader's sharp tone and annoyance, as he grudgingly granted her request to join the caravan. She also remembered his impatience before they departed and the unreadable expression in his gaze as he watched her wander the camp earlier in the day. She expected that fear for his people formed the root of his displeasure. She could not blame him. With a deep, slow breath, she willed the tension to run out of her. She gathered up her things, brushed the dirt and bits of tree bark off her butt, and followed Sveta toward the wagon Markos had entered earlier.

The sounds of the bustling camp punctuated by the laughter of both children and adults comforted her. The calm, easy way Sveta chatted with her, telling her little details about the clan and its people as they passed, comforted her. The approaching conversation? That made her uneasy. Whatever the conversation she was to have with Markos consisted of, Kara would keep her promise to Granddame Rose.

As they entered the cool dimness of the wagon Kara fought not to laugh as Beag Scath—still in his true form—scampered up her back to hide beneath her hair. Clearly, something of her amusement showed on her face, however, given Markos's deepening glower.

He did not offer her a seat on the bench across from him.

Only when the door quietly clicked closed behind her did Kara realize Sveta had left the wagon.

After a long moment of silence, Markos spoke, "I am honor-bound to give you a place among us. Do not believe for a moment I am happy about that. Through your actions one of our own is dead, and another broken."

Kara's heart clenched at the reminder and she reached up to finger the copper pendant Rose had given her as a protection against evil. It had become a touchstone for her. She did not dispute his claim, though Tony's situation was no fault of her own. Her time among the *Sidhe* had not exactly been peaceful or without strife. Quite the opposite, in fact, or she wouldn't be here. She nodded but remained silent.

"You are not a guest here, but you are not Clan. We have given you the place that was offered. In exchange, you will help where you are asked, and you will respect our ways. You will not intrude where you are not invited." His bright blue gaze speared her until she nodded, then he went on. "If you bring trouble to my people, we will consider honor met and you will leave."

She could not blame his bluntness. She knew exactly where it came from. Beag Scath, on the other hand, seemed to take offense, coiling beneath the fall of her hair until she worried what he might do. Placing a restraining hand over him, she nodded again. "Understood. Family before all others."

Markos looked stunned that she would know the mantra by which the Romani lived, and, beneath that, she may have seen a glimmer of respect hidden in his gaze. Rather than respond, though, he went back to whatever he was working on before she'd entered.

Clearly dismissed, Kara lowered her hand and turned to the door.

Before she knew it Beag Scath had pushed his way through the back of her hair and blew a prodigious raspberry all over Markos.

Kara looked back, ready to apologize. Instead, she choked on a laugh at the expression on Markos's face, a spectacular blend of amusement and outrage. Fortunately, amusement won out.

As the clan leader unleashed an equally prodigious belly laugh, Kara smiled and took her leave.

As she returned to Sveta's wagon, Kara noticed a vardo set aside from the others. Unlike the rest of the caravan, it was not in as good repair, its paint faded and peeling, the carving worn and damaged in places. Even to one unfamiliar with such things it looked ill-maintained.

"We had to scramble to find a place for him. That was all that was available."

Kara turned as Sveta came up next to her, frowning as she realized the woman spoke of Tony.

"His *puridaia's*..." The woman grimaced as she clearly grasped Kara would not know the word. "His *grandmother's* things had to be burnt, lest we invite her *mulo* among us to wreak retribution for any of life's slights, spirits hold grudges much longer than the living."

Sveta went on, her words lilting and accented, but in no way halting. "We were not expecting this one, and could not ask any of the clan to bear the risk of taking him in. That vardo came from outside the clan, long stored away by one who left off traveling. The men will take turns driving it until *that one* comes around enough to drive himself."

Despite the warmth of the afternoon sun, a chill settled over the glade where they stood. Kara tensed and pressed her lips closed tight, before she spoke her mind and offended the woman again when things were just becoming comfortable between them.

Before Kara could ask any of the half-dozen questions crowding her mind, Sveta nodded and turned away. Kara noticed the woman make an odd little gesture in Tony's direction as she moved on, no doubt a sign to ward off evil.

Outrage took hold of Kara's heart. While she understood the Rom's reluctance to associate with a man who had once been a vessel for pure evil, there was injustice in shunning him, when he was just as much the victim, if not more so.

Kara frowned, her gaze locked briefly on the wagon before following Sveta.

The wagon looked deserted. Kara had watched all morning. No one had come or gone from it. The Romani might have claimed Tony from the *Sidhe*, but none among them cared for him. Heck, Sveta wouldn't even say his name. Only now, looking more closely at the wagon, Kara noted various charms had been hung from any available protrusion and symbols to contain evil likewise marked wherever the carving allowed. None of them held power that Kara could see. What the Rom did not seem to grasp is that charms *guarding* against evil already decorated the wagon. The symbols carved when the vardo was made were imbued with mage power. Old and faded, but still strong.

If Tony were evil, he never could have entered the damned wagon, to begin with.

Anger kindled hot and heavy in her breast. Tony was a *victim*. Foolish, perhaps. A delinquent who unwittingly invited the trouble that had been visited upon him, most certainly. But nothing about him as a person was evil. Kara knew this. Intimately. She had seen evil, been touched by it. *Banished it*. Destroying Olcas and his brothers had been a good start to keeping her vow to Granddame Rose, but it wasn't enough when Tony's spirit remained shackled. Not when his own people had clearly cast him out in all but deed.

Time to get to work.

She returned to the wagon she shared with Sveta and her young sons and gathered what cleaning supplies she could find, leaving a twenty on the table. When she stepped back outside, Beag Scath appeared at her feet. The fierce scowl on the sprite's face reflected her own heart. Together they crossed the camp to the ancient-looking vardo where Rose's grandson was housed. Kara knocked. No one answered, but the ill-latched door opened beneath her hand. Stale, musty air wafted out, causing Kara to cough as she peered within. The interior was dark as twilight, and nothing moved. In the faint light, she spied a man-shaped form huddled on the far bunk beneath a moth-eaten blanket. Part of her marveled at how he'd folded his 5'10" frame so small; most of her fumed at his living conditions.

Kara set Quicksilver and her supplies beside the door and stepped inside. She opened the two shutters at either end to let in fresh air, and then returned outside to deal with the exterior of the wagon. It took several minutes and no small amount of clambering by herself and Beag Scath to strip away most of the charms. Those left had been crudely painted on and would need to be scrubbed off. Still, it was a start. Squaring her shoulders and setting her jaw, she pivoted and headed for the communal fire at the center of the camp. Without a word to anyone, but challenge in her gaze, she dumped the charms into the flames and returned to Tony's vardo.

There was not much else she could do about the condition of the wagon, but she would not give up on the man inside.

Returning to the main camp she approached the nearest vardo where one of the women, Susan Simko, prepared a meal. The herb-laden aroma of stewed lamb and vegetables set Kara's stomach rumbling.

"Please, may I have a portion?" Kara asked, respectful, but determined, holding the woman's gaze, daring her to look away.

"*Mizhak*," Susan muttered as she spat into the dirt, her gaze clearly on Tony's wagon. There was no doubt of her meaning.

"No," Kara answered, her tone polite, but forceful. "Broken, not wicked. *Family*."

She had no doubt the woman understood her words...and her determination.

Spitting again, Susan glared but shoved a smooth wooden bowl in Kara's direction before disappearing into her wagon, slamming the door behind her. Holding the bowl with one hand, Kara took up the ladle hanging over the cook pot with the other and scooped out a single modest portion of the savory stew before hanging up the ladle again.

"Thank you," she called out to the woman inside before carefully carrying the meal back to Tony's wagon. When she reached her destination, she looked back only to see Susan not only dump out the remainder of the meal but throw both the pot and ladle away. Kara frowned and felt the bite of guilt deep in her belly. The Rom were proud people, without much in the way of worldly goods. Kara had forgotten they had very strong beliefs. And superstitions. She would not make the same mistake again. Tonight, she would ask Sveta what arrangements had been made to meet Tony's needs, while allowing the others in the caravan to feel protected.

Mentally pushing up her sleeves, she went inside.

The bundle on the bed had cocooned tighter.

Kara set the bowl down on a massive wooden spindle that had been bolted to the floor as a table. She then moved to the bed and gently pulled the scratchy woolen blanket away.

Tony's head whipped up, his face drawn and pale, framed by dark, unruly curls that had started to grow out of the neat style he'd worn in New York. He glared at her with dark, bloodshot eyes, dull and slightly glassy. As he realized who she was, he paled even further, his hand shaking as it reached up to tug the blanket back. She didn't let him.

"Come on," she said as if nothing were off at all. "Time to eat."

Silently, he rose and did as she bid.

"That was a ballsy thing you did."

Kara nearly dropped the bucket she was carrying. As it was, fresh, bitter-cold spring water sloshed all over her jeans plastering them to her legs. She fought not to scowl as she looked up at the young woman with golden brown hair and deep brown eyes. Eyes that laughed and danced, even if the woman otherwise restrained the impulse.

"Sorry," the woman said, as she reached out a hand. "May I help?"

"Thanks, but I've got it," Kara told her without stopping, not feeling particularly charitable toward the Rom at the moment. Besides, she didn't have time to chat. With Tony fed, she needed to clean the wagon before she went to find her own meal. She continued to walk, Quicksilver bouncing against her back as the bucket weighed on her arms, expecting the woman would likely back off when she saw where Kara was heading.

Instead, the woman fell into step.

"My name is Linda, but they call me La-La."

"La-La?"

This time the woman did not hold back her laugh. The rich, throaty sound called a brief smile to Kara's lips though she didn't particularly feel cheerful at the moment. "My nieces and nephews started it, and everyone else just seemed to pick it up. At this point, I hardly expect anyone remembers I was once called Linda."

That made as much sense as anything else to Kara, and, really, it was unimportant. Her brow drew together as the woman's first words came back to her. "What was ballsy?"

La-La nodded ahead of them toward the wagon, still unkempt, but now unburdened by the charms that had adorned it. "Taking a stand...showing such compassion, when everyone else only shows fear. He has a long road ahead of him. You will mostly ease the way, except when you make it harder."

The words were like a pat on the back and slap in the face all at once. Too worked up to be diplomatic, Kara stopped and turned on the woman. "And leaving him to rot in a dank, broken-down wagon would be any better? It was the right thing to do! He needs taking care of, not shunning! Not one thing about that man is evil, except perhaps his memories, and those are none of his own doing."

"*Kushti, kushti...*" La-La said in a gentle tone, her hand raised as if to soothe. "*All right...*I know."

Kara's first impulse was to bristle, until La-La's words sank in. "You know?"

La-La nodded, her cheeks flushed and her gaze dropping briefly. "I am different. I See what others cannot."

By her emphasis, Kara understood. "Visions..."

Again, La-La nodded. "You are also special. A good woman for a *Rakli*, and..."

"*Kara*...my name is Kara..."

"Well, one of them is," La-La interrupted, her gaze knowing and her tone matter-of-fact.

Unsettled, Kara turned abruptly and continued walking.

"Please! Don't be upset," La-La called after her. "I wish only to be friends."

"What does *Rakli* mean?"

Again La-La flushed. "Sorry, no offense was meant. The word means a non-Romani girl."

"Well, I can hardly argue with that." Kara looked down at where her hand still clenched around the plastic bucket handle.

"As for the rest, please don't say anything. I expect if the others knew, they might have more of a hard time with me than they already do."

La-La got an odd look on her face, and, for a moment, her eyes seemed unfocused. Then she nodded. "I agree. I'll keep this between us unless I See someone must know."

Kara sighed. At least, La-La had been honest with her.

"Good day to you both," the Romani woman said as she turned to go her own way.

Tension coiled in Kara's gut. "Both?"

La-La looked back, her head cocked, and her lips quirked as her eyes flickered toward Quicksilver. "*Both.* Or have you already forgotten that I See?"

Kara grimaced inward, not sure she was comfortable with anyone else knowing of Danu's presence. It was one of the reasons she rarely went anywhere without the violin across her back.

Her discomfort must have shown. She sighed as La-La gave her an understanding look.

"She comes out and dances when you play," the woman said, mimicking the act. "No more than a pale shimmering outline hinting at her beauty. Sometimes her features align with your own in a near-perfect echo, and I see her more clearly." La-La's gaze grew pensive, and she drew a shuddering breath. "Such power, such love, and yet just a fragment of the whole. It fills me with awe to consider the depth of both, were the essence of the spirit complete."

Kara considered the woman's words, uncertain of how to respond.

La-La didn't wait for Kara to figure it out.

As the woman started to walk off once more, she turned back and nodded at Kara's clinging wet jeans. "You'll want to swap those out for long skirts as soon as you can, it will ease your path with the folk."

With that La-La smiled and waved before going her way.

The *Bás* fidgeted and fussed, hidden in the crevices of the host, riding it like a beast. As she went, she sipped on the host's soul, made savory with the fear and terror flooding it. Without a well of power to draw from, feeding on the host was more like lapping a trickle of water than supping on thick rich blood, but it sustained the *Bás* adequately for now. She conserved her strength and planned their vengeance. Through the bond of her kind, she knew others had survived the slaughter; and they knew the trick she had discovered of hiding within not-prey.

The cursed ones would not find them so easily.

They would not slaughter the *Bás's* young.

They would not see the death stroke as it came for them.

This made the *Bás* twitch even more with eagerness.

And as the host wended its way through the wilderness, the *Bás* discovered something else that had her and her sisters poised and ready to pounce. All the tiny soul streams that confused the hunt, all the tiny drips of faeling power that had muddled the trail of the cursed ones since the time of Danu— the *Cursed One* above all cursed ones—something had sucked the strongest of them up.

The *Sidhe*...the *Daoine Maithé* ...the *Tuatha de Danaan*....by whichever name the cursed ones called themselves, they could no longer hide as well as they once had.

When the *Bás's* numbers built again, the cursed ones would remember the fear of being prey.

The *Bás* went still as the host stopped to rest. She extended her senses and would have opened her mouth to scent the air, if she had been able. Even so, what she sensed nearly jolted her from her hiding place. No knowledge was ever lost to the *Bás*. What one knew, the others knew, all the way back to the dawn of time. Somewhere nearby, this *Bás* sensed a familiar essence she could scarce believe: Danu herself. Nearby and drawing closer.

She hissed, though the effort was less than satisfying through the host's blunt teeth and weak lips. Hunger and frustration filled her. There was nothing the *Bás* longed for more than vengeance against those called Anu and Danu, who together had brought millennia of misfortune upon them. Giving in to the frustration, this Bás slashed at her host, body and soul, devouring the shreds torn loose, not bothering to restrain herself when the host slumped over and her heart ceased to beat.

Chapter Two

Tony DeLocosta was no longer a boy. He'd never been an angel.

He was a man, a scarred and broken man. A prisoner within himself. No amount of magic could heal a victim's soul overnight.

Kara knew this intimately.

Tony had not even begun to recover from his ordeal, in many ways much worse than anything Kara had suffered at Olcas's hand. He would need help. Loved ones surrounding him, familiar, everyday tasks to distract him, someone who knew the path out of the darkness to show him the way. Someone who understood the silences, the brooding, the bleak hopelessness, the sudden lashing out...

And after all that, he'd need someone to teach him, for Tony was also mage born.

Right now, all he had was her. That wasn't working out well for either of them. While she had walked his path and understood, she also fed his shame.

She still slept in Sveta's vardo but had taken to traveling in Tony's wagon when the caravan hit the road. It had been almost a week. They barely spoke. Hell, Tony would scarcely even acknowledge her or anyone else. When she did manage to catch his eye, his gaze swam with guilt and quickly darted away.

Kara watched him now from the front of the wagon. He perched on the back ledge, one long leg dangling outside the window, the other knee bent, with his foot flat on the ledge. Months ago she had watched another Rom sit thus, confident but alert, balanced; Tony sat in a fog, carelessly, as if he didn't care about—or likely even perceive—the potential for injury...or worse.

Or did he tempt death?

Kara closed her eyes briefly against that thought. At one time, she would have gladly helped him find it. Even now, her emotions twisted and swirled like a tempest within her, clashing with reason. Though she knew that Olcas had controlled his hand, hatred lingered in her heart for Tony's face, which she could not separate from the memories of her torture and subsequent curse. The face Olcas had doomed her to see on every man she'd looked on *after*—and feel his touch—until Rose had broken the spell. And yet, Kara felt compassion for Tony's warm brown eyes—different from Olcas's cold, icy blue—which she'd yet to see steeped in anything except confusion or torment. Somehow, despite all that, beyond any comprehension, a seed of friendship had taken root. Both New Yorkers, both victims of the same evil force. Both freed yet still fighting demons. It pained her to think of Tony wishing for death...passively seeking it, even.

While Kara wasn't completely comfortable with this Romani man, she would not condemn him for deeds she *knew* were not his. Perhaps she could not heal him, but she could show him the way out of the deep dark hole swallowing him up. And then, she would be free to follow wherever her heart led.

Rising from the bench where she'd been staring out a side window, Kara reached into the cupboard for Quicksilver. The latch *snick*ed as she closed and secured the door. Tony did not even tense, let alone look back in reaction to the sound. Keeping her motions relaxed and easy, Kara made her way to his side, nudging his perched leg into the wagon under the pretext of joining him on the ledge. She kept both legs planted on the floor and canted her body so that she faced her companion. Firmly settled, she removed the violin from its case. Her soul brushed briefly against its other half but did not engage the essence of the goddess Danu. Kara tuned Quicksilver and brought the violin into position beneath her chin. She laid bow to strings and let the music and magic loose on the breeze, not guiding either, but letting them flow freely from tune to familiar tune as a spiritual balm. Though he did not acknowledge her presence... did not, in fact, even bring his eyes off the road scrolling out beneath the wagon's wheels...Tony subtly relaxed, his foot tapping softly in rhythm to her song.

And thus, with the smallest step, their shared journey to healing began.

Before too long, Kara found staying in the cramped quarters of Sveta's vardo more than trying. No room, no privacy, three squabbling boys...not easy to take for an only child used to plenty of space of her own. Without comment or question, she gathered her things one day and took over the spare bunk in Tony's wagon. Perhaps no more comfortable than where she had been, but certainly more quiet.

The further they traveled away from the *Sidhe* lands, the more Kara's nerves crawled, and her muscles bunched. At times it was because she sensed the *Tuatha de Danaan* out in the world around her. At others, it was because she didn't, and she wondered if something had gone wrong. Mostly, it was because she caught a phantom scent on the breeze, a hint of sharp musk that may or may not have been from memory...or more likely her nightmares. It reminded her of the *Namhaid*, ancient spirit-beings allied with the demigod, *Dubh*...the Black One, brother to Olcas. The creatures were beautiful but deadly. Those she had seen appeared like women with velvety white pelts and deep crimson hair, delicate fangs, brutal claws, and blood-red eyes. They moved like the great hunting cats in human form and were just as apt to toy with their prey. Her stomach churned at the memories. The *Namhaid* devoured souls; worse yet, they planted their young within the mage-born. After the defeat of the *Tuatha de Carman*, the Smithgod had sent his Hounds...his warriors, to route the *Namhaid* out and destroy them. She had no idea if they had been successful.

Kara shuddered and blew her breath through her nose in an attempt to dislodge the scent. She tried to throw off the pall the memories cast over the day but found it near impossible with nothing to distract her. Tony was still disinclined to speak with her and staring out over the changing landscape as the caravan traveled did nothing to divert her. With the past months brought to the forefront of her thoughts, Kara found herself sharing her own torment with Tony, fairly certain he would not betray the confidence.

In the heavy silences, she spoke of her ordeal, the violence done to her by the *Tuatha de Carman,* the mental anguish of her spell-bound torture, the struggle to fight past all of that to free herself, when impulse sent her fleeing to the darkest depths of her psyche.

"I couldn't dwell on their crimes, only my weakness, my inability to stand against them." She fell silent a moment, still fighting that sense of inadequacy, of helplessness that led to hopelessness. All false. All another offense to lay at the feet of Olcas and his brothers.

"Did you know," Kara asked in tones lower than a whisper, feeling as if her heart bled, "that I killed someone I loved…"

At that, Tony's head jerked around, and the fog lifted from his expression as his scowl deepened, along with the torment in his gaze. He'd been there, helplessly in thrall to Olcas's will, and shared that memory with her of the moment where Kara had killed her "Aunt" Lynn…or the demon who had taken over her form, anyway. Such particulars meant little in the middle of the night when it was Lynn Barnert Kara saw bleeding out in her dreams. Anguish etched deep furrows alongside Tony's mouth at the reminder, while annoyance quirked his lips. Not that he could have stopped any of it, but Kara could see it was one more thing that tormented him. Not her actions, necessarily, but what had come after, when she had been gut-shot and left for dead. He didn't speak, but she could sense his impulse first to fight, then to argue.

A sad, gentle smile flitted across her lips, and then was gone. "You're thinking it's not the same, that it wasn't her anymore. I know, I'm not denying that or trying to snow you…but it's not so easy to tell my heart that. The guilt weighs on me regardless. I understand, but I can't help what I feel, right?" Any more than Tony could, when he remembered the sword-thrust that ended his grandmother's life. The one Olcas guided using Tony's hand.

The silence took on more weight as that realization hung in the air. The light seemed to dim, the shadows darken. Kara watched the muscles of Tony's face grow tight until they faintly twitched beneath his right eye.

"I do understand," she murmured once more, as she deliberately caught his gaze. She would not tell him not to feel what he felt. Not only was that wrong and ultimately more harmful, but it was asking for the impossible.

Without another word she rose, returning Quicksilver to the cabinet before stretching out on the bunk to nap, leaving Tony caught between reason and emotion.

For the first month, most of the adult members of the caravan did not speak a word to Kara that was not instruction or in Romani, of which she still had no practical knowledge beyond the few words she'd learned from La-La or the children. Most of the time, she scarcely noticed, lost as she was in her own thoughts and concerns. Tony had slowly begun to open up, but not much. Mostly, he grunted in a gruff, you're-a-pain-in-my-ass kind of way when she wouldn't leave him alone, but, occasionally, he voiced a few words in blessed English, mostly to warn her away from doing something stupid that would result in broken goods or broken skin.

Soon after she'd started traveling in his wagon, he dragged himself from his bunk and took over the driver's seat, releasing the other men from their enforced rotation. Clearly, he did it to avoid being confined with her more than necessary. Kara didn't mind. It was good for him to make the effort, to get outside himself and outside period. Even if his persistent silence made her crazy at times.

She would be patient and strive for perseverance. After all, she had not joined the caravan just for herself but to help Tony. Though her presence alone proved a hindrance at times, she could not give up, certainly not because of a little thing like feeling out of place. It was hardly the first time she had coped with that.

It was not as if the Rom made her feel unwelcome—with the understandable exception of Tony from time to time—but they were a private people. Once they had gotten past expecting

Tony to turn on all of them, they relaxed and ignored Kara's connection to him. They were polite enough to her but still kept their distance. To be fair, she expected they weren't sure what to make of her either. Whether La-La had let something slip or not, somehow they knew she was different, *other*, even if they didn't know how.

As Markos had warned, Kara was given chores to do. Menial tasks. Things that required little or no skill and even less explanation. Things that needed to be done but didn't exactly occupy her mind or fill her day, though often they did leave her achy. She spent hours collecting and stacking firewood or spreading dry straw over ground gone muddy and wet, carrying things that needed cleaning down to the nearest stream or river for others to scrub. In her free time, she had taken it upon herself to help the children with their chores. They were more than delighted to let her. Kara enjoyed being with them and had even picked up a few more words in Romani. Not much. Not enough to hold an adult conversation, but she could certainly name a fair number of things. Or she thought she could, anyway.

For all she knew, they'd taught her curse words.

This afternoon, she and the children roamed along a creek and the nearby woods gathering herbs. The crisp green scent mingled with the aroma of rich loam delighted Kara's nose even as the laughter of the children soothed her soul.

"This one is for tummy aches," Sadie, the littlest of the herb hunters, told Kara. She then said the name in Romani and showed Kara what to gather and how to do so. "And this one makes the lamb taste extra good." It was hard not to laugh at the child's serious manner in contrast to the way she skipped from plant to plant, bounding like a little goat.

"And what does this one do?" Kara asked, reaching for a curious plant with spiky leaves and a tall umbrella-shaped cluster of little white flowers.

Sadie gasped and swatted Kara's hand away. "That one burns you *real* bad."

Kara started to chuckle at the way the girl's eyes went big and wide, her words so earnest, until she realized how upset Sadie actually was.

One of the older children came up behind them. "Good job, Sadie Rae," Maddox said, and ruffled the girl's golden brown curls, before turning to Kara. "Best not to touch anything you don't know unless one of us says it's safe. That one's giant hogweed. Touch that and you'd break into a rash that burns and blisters." He pulled out a cell phone—which Kara so hadn't expected—and called up a picture on his web browser. She shuddered and quickly looked away.

Before she could thank them, yelling and banging and loud crashes rose from the direction of the camp. All of the children stopped and turned toward the sound before suddenly scrambling for places to hide. Kara would have headed for the clearing if not for Maddox tugging her back. He held his finger to his lips and drew her into the brush where they huddled in silence.

When fifteen minutes had passed Maddox's phone silently lit up, alerting to an incoming text. "Okay, everybody, let's head back," the boy said quietly. "Piper…'Rayah…come on. Logan, help the little ones."

Unsettled, Kara watched a boy a year or two younger than Maddox gather up the bundles the littlest children struggled with. His soulful eyes were dark and angry and just a bit scared. Kara joined him in claiming their burdens. She then took Sadie's hand in her own and followed without a word as the other children gathered their things and their findings and marched back to camp. Her heart ached at how solemn their mood had grown.

The moment they came into the clearing, the kids hurried to their respective wagons, but Kara stopped abruptly. The current camp was in a wide meadow between a wooded area and the road, about five miles outside of Carmarthen, Wales, according to La-La. Several of the wagons closest to the road had been toppled on their sides, the others bore large splatters of black or red paint.

"What the…!" Kara gasped, not knowing what to do.

When she reached for one of the cushions that had gone tumbling, one of the Rom glowered at her and snatched it away. Yanking her hand back, Kara wrapped her arms around herself and went to sit on the steps of Tony's wagon. Clearly, her help was not welcome. She watched as the Rom set the camp back to order; the women gathering up the goods, and the men righting the wagons. Quicker than Kara would have expected, all sign of the disruption was gone, except where tires had torn up the grass between the camp and the road. Even the paint had been washed away with well-practiced efficiency. All in utter silence.

"Why?" she murmured to herself. "For goodness sake, why?"

"Sometimes, the townies don't like it when we set up camp nearby."

Kara startled. She hadn't realized La-La had come up beside her. She looked up at her friend as she leaned against the wagon. La-La's beautifully embroidered blouse and ruffled skirt were ruined, spattered with great splotches of paint. Some of it also matted her hair.

Kara was torn between sorrow and outrage. Hate was nothing new in the world, and certainly not in Kara's experience, but this was different. Groundless and petty. Brutal, out of nowhere. It disgusted her. "We haven't even seen two cars drive by. Why do they care? It's not like you set up right outside of town!"

La-La made a scoffing laugh and pushed her golden brown hair behind her ear. "Sometimes, the townies don't like it when we breathe the same air. Who's to explain? There will always be those who distrust the *other*. And sometimes they are right to...but mostly not. Or at least not for the reasons they do. There is no point trying to make sense of the senseless."

Kara jerked a bit at that, having recently thought the Romani had similar issues regarding her. She said nothing, though, and just shook her head. Then she frowned as she noticed the cushions and rugs and colorful drapes that made the outdoor sitting spaces being packed away, rather than just being put to rights. "Are they breaking camp already? We just got here..."

Before La-La could answer, Tony came striding up, his tee shirt soaked with sweat and stained from helping to right the wagons. She almost smiled to see him out among others, until she caught the earthy pong of shit wafting around him as well. Apparently more than paint had been thrown. He looked understandably distant, his words both hollow and angry as he spoke. "Only a fool invites more trouble. There are other fields. Other towns."

One of the men called out his name before he could go on. Grimacing, Tony turned back to her. "Secure the wagon for me and get it ready to go. I have to help round up the ponies."

Until he said something, Kara hadn't realized the animals had been scattered.

She nodded. "Go on, I'll take care of it."

Only Tony was already gone.

Behind her, La-La hummed in appreciation. "Your husband looks real good in a wet tee shirt, even one smeared with dung."

Kara spun around so fast she nearly fell off the steps as La-La's words hit her. Her lips went numb, and she felt her eyes go wide in panic.

"No! No-no-no!" She couldn't get anything else out, but La-La must have realized what she wanted to say.

"Oh...well, don't tell anyone else that. The only reason they didn't raise a fuss when you moved into his wagon is they thought he took you to wife. Tell them otherwise, and they'll shun you as impure...or worse."

The world spun around Kara as she clutched the step beneath her to remain upright.

No-no-no-no-no!

It was nearing evening by the time Tony returned to the wagon. It had been over an hour since Kara had brought in and stowed what little they had set up outside and buttoned up the loose items inside. She heard him hitching up their pony but could not bring herself to go and help. When Tony came through the door, she was waiting for him, sitting on his bunk with her hands fisted in his blankets. She shot to her feet the moment the door closed, so upset she barely recoiled as he loomed over her.

"What the hell, Tony?!"

"What's wrong now?"

"They think we're *married!*" Kara hissed. She could hear the echo of her earlier panic in her voice, but she couldn't help it.

Tony flinched as if she'd hit him, his muscles tensing as he went stock still.

"Why do you care? You know the truth. I know the truth. What does it matter what they believe?" Buried beneath the indifference, she thought she heard pain in his voice. She wished she could see his eyes to know for sure.

"What if they find out?"

"You're the one that moved in," he added, a sneer twisting his lips as he leaned close. "You don't like it, move out...maybe they'll *assume* you divorced me."

This time Kara flinched, though she fought not to. With that expression on his face and his eyes hidden from her, it was like looking at Olcas once more.

Tony cursed, clearly picking up on her reaction. This time there was no mistaking the pain.

"Decide now. It's time to leave," he snapped, his tone flat and dull as he spun away and left the wagon. The whole thing shifted subtly from side to side as he climbed up into the driver's seat.

Kara plopped back down on his bunk as Tony waited a moment, then started the wagon rolling with a jerk.

Why *did* she care? Damned if she knew...or maybe she did and just wouldn't admit the reason, even to herself.

Somewhere between Carmarthen and the English country-side, Kara rebelled, tired of seeing little but the inside of the caravan. One day, after they had stopped to water both ponies and people, she climbed up onto the driver's seat beside Tony. She returned him scowl for scowl until he blinked and looked away. Kara couldn't swear to it, but she was pretty sure she saw the hint of a smile tug at his lips. Fleeting but encouraging. Things were still a little tense between them, but they had settled into a more comfortable peace. Just two New Yorkers in a Romani world. They didn't speak about their little blow-up. Not wanting to examine why she panicked, Kara let it go. Clearly, no one else had an issue, which was saying a lot for the Romani, so why should she?

Kara looked over at Tony and smiled. Overall, she was pleased with the progress he had made. No longer as withdrawn, no longer completely closed off. Despite her freak-out, something had changed after the attack on the caravan, when everyone came together to put things right. Or maybe it was that she hadn't taken Tony's suggestion and walked out on him. Whatever the reason, even the members of the caravan had noticed. And the more Tony relaxed, the more they did. With each day that passed, there were fewer gestures against evil or wary glances.

Not to say all was well with the Kalderaš Clan, but it was a start.

They drove along for hours in silence, save for the sound of wagon wheels and clopping hooves. Neither of them knew where the caravan was headed, but it scarcely mattered with the wagons stretched out before them in a trail impossible not to follow.

The steady, rocking pace lulled them until sudden cries rose ahead. Kara jerked upright, as did Tony beside her. He signaled the ponies to stop and glanced at her as if about to tell her to stay where she was. Kara shot him a glare and climbed down to the ground before he could decide to use actual words. A sharp Romani curse followed her, with Tony trailing right after. They walked past the other wagons until they reached where Leona Wisoker stood holding her pony's bridle, stroking him as if to soothe, though the placid pony was considerably calmer than she seemed to be.

Tony stopped beside the woman.

He spoke to her in the Romani tongue, nearly all traces of Brooklyn gone from his voice. Kara didn't understand a word of what he said but the musical tones did something pleasant to her insides. Startled by her reaction, she looked away, scanning the road ahead trying to figure out what had stopped the caravan. Off to the side, near a copse of trees, several of the men knelt in the brush looking at the ground.

Something drew Kara to join them, her skirts swishing about her legs as her strides lengthened with a sense of growing urgency. Behind her, barely heard, Tony called out to her to come back, but he was too late. She came to a stop just behind the men, for a moment unnoticed.

She drew a sharp breath, and all of them spun, several rising to stand upright, while others just pivoted on their knee. All of them looked ready to defend themselves. On the ground before them lay the remains of a woman...a backpacker or hiker. They would never know which.

Once again Kara thought she caught a wisp of the *Namhaid*'s familiar pong on the air. Was it a subconscious suggestion? The gashes did vaguely remind her of the *Namhaid*. Brutal. Vicious. But something wasn't right. The injuries were too rough, lacking the razor-sharp precision characteristic of a *Namhaid* kill. These...they almost seemed...

Kyp Carter, one of the Rom that knelt, reached out but stopped just shy of touching the body. Instead, he traced the air just above the jagged wound then brought his hand up and raked his fingers through his blond hair.

"It's as if..." he murmured, forgetting himself and speaking in English. "It's as if the cuts came from the inside."

At his words, Kara shuddered violently. Once, she had seen a *Sidhe* corpse after *Namhaid* young had whelped from inside of it. The memories added to her nightmares, on occasion. This did not seem right compared to what she had seen before, but what if she was wrong? What if instead of being eradicated, these predators had eluded Goibhniu's Hounds in some unnatural way?

"No," she gasped. None with the mage gift would be safe.

She started as Tony grabbed her arm from behind to pull her away. Biting off a growl, he propelled her back to their wagon without a word, his expression livid and his olive complexion pale.

She did not resist as he marched her to the door and all but pushed her in. Before he could slam it shut, she put her arm out to hold it open, if only briefly.

"Tony..." she started before pausing to compose herself as she heard the tremor in her own voice. "Tony, I think it was the *Namhaid*."

Pain quaked across Kara O'Keefe's chest and down her limbs. Her back arched against bonds that were not there, and a shriek trembled at her lips, lacking only the breath to propel it. Her eyes snapped wide as she gasped for air. Once she had it, she turned her face into her pillow and let out the thwarted cry, knowing she must, or the need would plague her, growing and growing until the scream broke free no matter where she was or what she was doing.

She lay there in the dark with aftershocks of phantom pain rippling across her sweat-slick skin. She ignored them, her entire focus trained on breathing in and out in slow, even measure until the tightness in her chest loosened. The more she calmed, the more aware she became of the constant, soothing murmur deep in her consciousness where the link to Danu twined with Anu's...*her* soul. Even in slumber, the goddess sought to comfort her.

Mentally, Kara burrowed into that connection, banishing the last of her terror-born chills. With practiced discipline, she relaxed her muscles and slowly drew a hand under her nightclothes and over her breast, her belly, her thighs—flesh that rightly should have borne horrific mutilations. Her impulse was to catalog those vanished scars, but she forced her mind to focus on the smooth, unblemished reality, rather than the crippling poison of those memories.

As her spirit settled, Kara blew out a hard breath, banishing the last, lingering remnants of her nightmare. It had been months since she had had such a bad episode. But what else could she expect, given her...conversations with Tony? In an effort to heal him, she picked at her own scabs.

And then to find that poor woman... Kara closed the lid on that horror. Blowing out another breath, she again forced herself to relax each taut muscle and focus her senses on the world beyond herself.

Outside the vardo walls, she heard the low sleepy chirps of songbirds warming up to serenade the morning. Further away, someone tended the ponies, and someone else—according to Kara's nose—prepared bacon for breakfast. She let the sounds and scents soothe her until she felt the urge to get up and greet the day. There was no logic in laying there awake waiting for the rest of the caravan to stir. She sat up, intending to slide quietly from both her bunk and the wagon, when a strangled groan sounded beyond the curtain that gave them each some privacy.

Reaching out, she slid the curtain to the side. Tony lay rigid in his bunk. His knuckles stood out like white marble where he clutched the frame.

"I disturbed you…I'm sorry," Kara said softly, forcing herself to keep her eyes trained on his face, noting each subtle difference between Tony as himself and Tony as possessed by Olcas, the latter brutally fresh in her mind thanks to her recent nightmare.

Tony's head jerked, and he swallowed hard. "Yeah, you could say that," he said, turning away, but not before Kara noted his expression, jaw tight and eyes slightly wild.

"I am sorry. Do you want to talk about it?"

Tony glared back, baring his teeth with a growl, only to pale as fresh guilt shadowed his gaze. Groaning again, he flung himself out of his bunk, disappearing from her sight. The door to outside slammed almost immediately. Kara sighed.

Was it a mistake staying in such close proximity to him? Something deep inside said no, but, at moments such as this, Kara had to wonder. She had not expected such a vivid dream after so long without one.

Chapter Three

Needing some distance and time alone, that afternoon Kara decided to comb the nearby forest for firewood. Their stockpile grew low, and Tony did all the driving, so she tried to take up the rest of the slack by making sure the wagon was stocked with what they needed. She put some food in a sack, helped herself to one of Tony's utility knives, and slung Quicksilver across her back before heading out. She was careful to stay within shouting distance of the camp. It would be foolish not to, given what they'd found on the road. Her skin crawled at the memory. Again, she could swear she smelled the barest whiff of *Namhaid* musk.

Kara tensed as the twilight beneath the trees grew deeper, peering more into the gloom than at the ground, and gathering precious little wood.

If the *Namhaid* had returned, all mage-touched were at risk. Kara needed to warn the *Sidhe*. But how?

As she searched for deadfall, soft, familiar murmurings caught her attention. Faelings crept from the trees, drawing close then darting away. One peered at her from the brush; his dark curls tight and close, and his expression somehow both distant and more intense. He cocked his head as he considered her then drew back into the foliage.

Kara watched him closely, her brow drawn in, perplexed by his behavior, so atypical. She would have moved closer if not for the other faelings flocking toward her. Smiling, she knelt for them, holding still lest she startle away the more skittish ones. She spied a gnome or two, and several sprites, while a bold pixie hovered around her head before lighting on her shoulder.

"Well hello, my miss," Kara murmured to her.

The pixie tittered and brushed a kiss across her cheek, leaving behind a dusting of sparkles. Wary of being out too long, and certainly not wanting to put the faelings at risk, she greeted each one and sent them on their way, feeling their presence recede as they sought out their nests. Too well she remembered what the *Namhaid* had done to their kin, leaving piles of broken faeling bodies as a message to the *Sidhe*. Kara clenched her jaw against the memory.

Never again.

That was when she remembered the odd little fellow.

Turning back toward the brush, she could just see him peeking out.

Sensing how timid he was, Kara lowered herself to the ground, her legs crossed Indian-style, with Quicksilver slung around to rest in her lap. Silently, she shooed Beag Scath away, for now, expecting the odd fellow might be shy. Once she was alone, she patiently waited. The little sprite came sauntering out, his motions more powerful than his counterparts, more stiff, less delicate and dancelike. He stopped right before her and canted his head once more.

"Hello, little one..." Kara murmured.

"Heya!" he answered, but his gaze rested on Quicksilver, not Kara. His expression was one of intrigue. "Where's the rest of you?"

Kara felt her face twist up in confusion.

"T.Rob," he said, this time clearly talking directly to her, though he would not meet her eye.

"I'm sorry?"

"T.Rob...not little one, thank you." He fidgeted, bobbing a bit as he spoke.

Kara found herself canting her head much the way T.Rob had. While it wasn't unheard of for sprites to talk, they rarely did, more often singing words, if they used them at all. T.Rob seemed altogether different from others of his kind. In fact...in fact, he reminded her an awful lot of one of her old students, from her days of teaching at the Music Center back in Queens, a musically gifted, high-functioning autistic girl named Patsy.

"You're all put back together," the sprite said, his tone chiding. "Now it's her turn..."

Without another word T.Rob turned and hurried away, disappearing altogether in the underbrush.

Kara frowned and shook her head, not knowing what to make of the encounter. Something he said did inspire her, though, if not in the way he'd intended.

The different pieces that made her—Kara-Anu—what she was had indeed come together. She kept forgetting that and all she was now capable of.

Beag Scath's soul brushed her own in a coy query if he could return, a reminder that her connection to the magical world extended well beyond faelings, the children of her soul. She was capable of communicating with the others of her kind in a way her strictly human self could never have contemplated.

Kara closed her eyes and reached her thoughts out to the *Tuatha de Danaan.* The awareness of the others was always there in the background, though she had taught herself to ignore the distraction. When she focused, though, she could easily sense her fellow *Sidhe.*

Hello, Kara soul spoke to her nearest kin.

"Hello," the other answered aloud and much closer than Kara had anticipated.

Kara's eyes snapped open, and her hand went to her utility knife. She relaxed, if only slightly, as her gaze came to rest on a slender maiden with pale opalescent skin and auburn tresses a few shades lighter than Kara's own. The *Sidhe* woman had pushed through the underbrush, her green tunic and grey-brown leggings making it seem she was one with the foliage. Eyes the color of a robin's egg danced as the woman waited patiently for Kara to respond.

Laughing, Kara blushed. "Sorry, I wasn't expecting you to join me."

"Then why ever did you summon me away from my herb-gathering?" the woman asked, a bit snappy.

With effort, Kara did not respond in kind. She'd forgotten how mercurial some of the kin could be. "I am Kara."

The woman inclined her head at the nicety. "You may call me Primrose."

"I bear a warning, Primrose, one that needs to be spread far and wide, all the way to *Mór Halla* and beyond; the *Namhaid* have not been banished. Tell Aí they hide within another."

The *Sidhe* woman's pale skin went a silvery grey at Kara's words. Primrose listened intently as Kara told her about the body the Rom had discovered. "The victim was not mage-born, but I smelled the creature's musk myself, and the marks where something clawed its way out were as near to a whelping as I can imagine, without a kit climbing from the corpse. Please, you must warn the kin."

As Kara finished, the *Sidhe* went still and taut, her eyes going wide as they focused just over Kara's shoulder. "You…It is you…" And abruptly, Primrose disappeared into the forest.

Confused, Kara turned to check what was behind her, only to see nothing but more trees. Only when she turned back and felt Quicksilver shift with her movement did she expect she knew what had sent Primrose hurrying away.

Apparently, their reputation preceded them, and Primrose didn't know how to handle the *Sidhe*-Who-Was-Not-*Sidhe*. Kara prayed the woman spread the word anyway, as Kara would continue to do every chance she got.

As Kara returned from the forest, Tony met her at the tree line, effortlessly scooping what wood she had gathered from her arms and depositing it in front of their wagon.

"You shouldn't wander off alone like that," he said gruffly.

"We needed wood." She then handed him his knife and started to walk past him.

He just gave her an odd look as he noticed the violin across her back. "You take that thing everywhere?"

Kara blushed. "She's a part of me."

He shook his head and grinned. Kara could almost hear his unspoken '*whatever.*' She didn't mind, though. This was the most unburdened she had seen him. Ever.

"Come on, you're in for a treat. Siege is here."

Kara's forehead wrinkled and one brow quirked. "Siege?"

Tony nodded, then tugged her arm, already turning away to draw her toward the fire where a large, white-maned man sat surrounded by a seething throng of children. He did not have the coloring of the Rom, but something in the way he held himself spoke of a similar larger-than-life presence. Kara liked the way his bright blue eyes sparkled in the firelight.

"Alright, already!" Kara heard him call out over the clamoring. "Sit down and shut up, or I'm goin' ta bed."

She marveled at the children's brief, gleeful shouts but more so at how quickly and thoroughly they complied. As they settled, she noted how many of the adults drew closer as well, nudging children to the ground and slipping onto the logs they had perched on.

Tony tapped a gangly pre-teen on the shoulder and nodded him toward the others, then waved Kara to where the boy had sat. Kara would have protested, if not for the expectant air that gripped them all. She looked over and smiled at the woman next to her, then leaned forward to say hi to the man on the woman's other side. They were Megan and Robert Wyatts, a sister and brother who shared the vardo across the clearing from Tony's. Megan was sweet and pretty, with long fiery red hair and a solid, athletic body. Her brother...he was a giant! Muscular and tall, as few others in the caravan were. Quiet, but kind.

Megan smiled back, Robert nodded, but neither of them said anything as they waited with an expectant air.

They weren't the only ones.

Kara looked around and could scarcely believe the silence as everyone present sat forward, rapt and waiting. Never in her travels with the Rom had she seen them so still...or quiet, not even in slumber. Before she could turn to ask Tony why the man at the center of it all began to speak.

And then Kara understood.

At some point, wonderstruck tears trickled down her cheeks. She had thought her grandda a gifted storyteller. This man... he put even the Smithgod Goibhniu to shame. The words, the characters, brief snippets of made-up song, they came alive on the breath of his rich baritone voice. Kara scarcely noticed the tale that he told; she was so drawn into the weft of his weaving.

On impulse, she slid Quicksilver's case around from where it lay across her back. Removing the violin, she tuned it and, urged by some inner sense, began to play a soft accompaniment as Siege started another tale.

Across the fire, she noticed him grin as his cadence flowed in harmony with her playing. Almost without notice, the music subtly transformed, its melody twining to follow the metronome of his voice.

Kara lost herself in the tune as the tune lost itself in the tale.

When all was done, and only the fire's crackling offset the silence, a faint tremor coursed her limbs as they drifted to her side, only lightly gripping the fiddle and bow. Not until the Rom erupted in cheers did Kara's chest swell with a swift-drawn breath. He was a master bard. And, she realized with a start, a fellow New Yorker. Again Kara's forehead furrowed. *What was he doing here?*

She turned to Tony and anything she might have asked faded from her thoughts. For the first time in months, the dark pall shrouding his soul had lightened.

Tony must have felt her gaze. He turned and smiled at her. "What?"

"Who is he, and where did he come from?"

That brought a laugh. "He's a rogue and a scoundrel, shameless and bold and wont to wander, but where he will and not at another's direction."

Kara laughed. "So poetic!"

"His words, not mine," Tony said. "He's an author. Makes a living driving a beat-up minivan from sci-fi convention to sci-fi convention telling his tales, selling his books, pinching pennies until they scream, and getting by on the kindness of friends and strangers."

"He's a New Yorker, what's he doing here? I can't imagine there are enough cons in Great Britain to keep him clothed, let alone fed!"

Tony frowned and confusion clouded his gaze.

"I don't know...I knew him in Brooklyn. I thought I'd heard he'd died, but..."

Kara looked across the fire at Siege, took in his mischievous gaze and great big rumbling laugh, his vitality and sheer presence. There was no one she had ever met who seemed more alive. And again he brought to mind her grandda...who'd died...but hadn't died...

She would not be surprised if Siege were gone in the morning, but for the joyous memories he left behind. After all, free spirits were wont to wander.

There were screams in the night, and they were not Kara's. She came instantly alert and rose from her bunk. Not again! Was it more 'townies' lashing out in fear and hate, or something worse? Scrambling from her cubby she nearly collided with Tony.

"That wasn't you."

Kara shook her head, but Tony had already flung himself out the wagon door, skipping the steps altogether as he hit the ground at a run, unconscious flickers of mage energy trailing behind him. The door slammed behind her as Kara followed. On impulse, she had grabbed Quicksilver on her way out, slinging the violin over her shoulder by the case's strap.

In the dark, shadowy figures hurried toward one of the wagons on the other side of the camp. The screams had ended, but the night was filled with shouts and calls of what Kara could only assume were instructions.

She really needed to properly learn Romani.

She slowed and hung back as she neared where everyone had clustered. These were not her people, after all. They would not welcome her intrusion. La-La wandered past. Even in the dark, Kara could tell her friend was pale and trembling.

"What is it, La-La? What happened?"

La-La stopped abruptly. Her eyes were unfocused, shocky, rolling almost manically. "So much...so much..."

Frowning, Kara reached out and drew her friend close. La-La's body went tense, rigid, even. Kara looked around hoping to find someone to explain. She spied Tony heading for them. His gaze flickered to the tee shirt and boxers she slept in. He scowled as he looked up again. When he drew close, Kara noticed his face was also ghostly white and his breath choppy. Her heart ached to see the haunted look return.

Instinctively, she reached out to him.

Tony waved her off and looked at her clothes again.

"Go get decent before someone sees you."

Kara glared at him. As far as she was concerned, she was decent. Besides, it wasn't as if she'd expected to come out into public. She bit back the urge to comment, though. She was among the Rom and, to them, the sight of her legs was *marime* ...dirty. And as her 'husband,' Tony would share her shame in their eyes. Annoyed, she went inside and pulled her skirt from earlier on over the boxers.

"Thank you," Tony murmured as she came back out. "Now please...you and the Lady, see if there's anything you can do..." He pointed toward the wagon across the way where the disturbance seemed to be localized.

Kara stared at him, her brow furrowed, not sure La-La would be much help to herself at the moment, let alone anyone else, but then Kara realized Tony's gaze went to the violin slung across her back. *Danu.* He meant Danu...or Quicksilver, anyway, for he couldn't know part of the goddess resided within. *Could he?*

Kara drew a sharp breath and hugged her friend tight. "I'll be back soon."

La-La stood like a board, without responding or reacting.

Whatever had happened must have been bad. With a gentle squeeze, Kara passed her to Tony's care and hurried for the group standing beside the wagon. It was not difficult to work her way past the milling crowd. Many hung back, their expressions a moving tapestry of horror, sorrow, and confusion. Common to all was an air of outrage. Hands flickered like pale flames in the darkness, over and over making signs against evil. Slowly, respectfully, Kara stepped past them and up to those by the wagon.

"You! This is your fault," a shrill voice called out from the crowd. "There has been nothing but bad luck since you joined us."

Kara turned and scanned the faces. Most were stunned and uncertain, but the speaker stood out. Sevilla Monroe. Her dark hair and eyes made her blend with the night, but the malice in her gaze burned like a beacon. The woman had never warmed to Kara. She was a fellow fiddle player and had no kindness for anyone who outshone her...particularly one not of the Rom.

It was an effort not to respond but Kara managed. She turned back to the crowd gathered beside the wagon. One look at the clan leader's face, however, and Kara was ready to tear out Sevilla's raven curls.

Markos glared at Kara, his jaw flexing and his lips twitching back. Remembering their talk, it was very likely he was about to cast her out, egged on, no doubt, by Sevilla's claims.

"Don't," Kara said. "I had nothing to do with this. I don't even know what *this* is."

From the look on Markos's face that might just be irrelevant at this point.

"I've come to see if I can help," she continued, keeping her tone low and even.

The clan leader stepped to the side and swept his hand toward the ground. "And how do you propose to help that?"

Kara gasped, and her thoughts went a little frantic at the sight of the man on the ground at her feet. *Robert...Robert Wyatts. What in the world could have brought this giant down?* His clothing gaped in long furrows from chest to groin, as did the flesh and muscle beneath. Blood glistened in the lamplight, and Kara caught a sharp, fetid odor that she suspected meant a bowel had been sliced. Was there something else? A hint of musk? Dear God, she hoped not. She hadn't thought beyond the mage-born *Sidhe.* It hadn't even occurred to her that any among the Rom might be at risk. She swallowed back the bile surging up her throat. Robert and his sister, Megan, had shared a seat with her just this evening. They had laughed and groaned and hung on Siege's words together.

"This isn't *Tir na nÓg.* Even those faerie-touched cannot help the dead."

Markos had a point.

"Where's Megan?"

"Inside...perhaps her you could help..." one of the women said.

Kara turned her gaze to the wagon, another traditional vardo, intricately carved and painted with runes and symbols of protection. Even to her normal vision, the symbols held a faint shimmer. Mage energy. Powerful mage energy. Kara's brow furrowed in confusion. Not Robert's or Megan's. She wondered who placed the protections...there was almost a *Sidhe* quality to the energy.

"They weren't inside, then," she murmured.

"No," the auld woman confirmed, though it had not been a question, and Kara had not particularly been talking to her. "They had been to tend to a sick pony and were just returning."

Kara looked at where the clan's ponies were tethered, then back to the woman. "Has anyone checked to see if the animals are unharmed? Or if anyone else has been attacked?"

Markos answered instead, his voice rife with annoyance. "Of course. No other has been harmed—man or beast."

Kara looked toward the entrance of the wagon. Several brawny men stood guard, though she wasn't sure why. From within the vardo, harsh curses and soulful cries mingled in the night, both sounding of one voice. The anguish drew her, even as some darker thread beneath it told her to flee. She ignored the impulse and nodded to the woman, but, when she turned to head for the wagon, a hand reached out to halt her, all whipcord and leather, with knobby joints that had to ache.

"Best you help from here if you can," the auld woman said.

Kara nodded. A mere wagon wall would make no difference. Either she could help, or she could not. She barely noticed La-La come up beside her as she removed Quicksilver from her case and prepared to play.

As if in response, the uproar grew more violent.

Pain and fear and anguish radiated from the wagon. Kara felt all three as if they burrowed into her heart. Hard behind that, sharp jags of rage spiked through everything, growing stronger.

Kara's eyes narrowed, and she swiftly raised her shields against the outside emotion wrestling away her control. The vardo shuddered and rocked as something slammed against the door from the inside. Her gaze jerked back to the wagon while, beside her, the elder gripped her arm again and shook.

"Play!" both she and Markos ordered Kara at once.

Before the imperious command faded, Kara ran bow across strings, her fingers already working up and down Quicksilver's neck. Her instructors at Juilliard would have stood in awe at the melody, goddess-guided and filled with the power of ancient magic, yet gentle and soothing as a mother's lullaby. Even the night creatures hushed. Kara focused her thoughts as Maggie had taught her, visualizing her music wrapping around the one suffering, guiding it to sooth the fears, dull the pain, and bring peace to the troubled soul within. It took many long minutes of her playing for the vardo to stop its shaking. The screams from inside gradually lost their shrill force, fading to sobs, then whimpers, and finally silence.

Kara continued to play, the tune drifting into a healing air.

The *Bás* sank her claws deep into the psyche of her new host. This one was almost-prey, possessing more power than most mortals, thready and thin though it was compared to the cursed ones. The *Bás* resisted the urge to consume the meager offering. This one had already brought her close to her chosen prey, if only briefly. Vengeance yet eluded her but not for much longer.

Age upon Age upon Age, her race had waited to strike down the rightful prey who cast the *Bás* into turmoil and near extinction.

Anu and Danu. Two cursed souls who for so long had been out of reach.

At last, this *Bás* had scented that long-sought prey, had seen the one called Danu...or her essence, anyway, housed within the instrument the other played.

She would bide her time and savor the hunt. Creeping close until the moment was right to lash out with fang and claw.

None stalked so well as the *Bás*.

Worn out, Kara walked in silence beside Markos as he escorted her back to the vardo. Internally, she struggled. Should she mention the *Namhaid* or would that only do more harm? What if she were wrong? Surely Markos would banish Kara if there were even a hint of more trouble connected with her, but, if she were gone, there would be none left among the clan who knew how to deal with the spirit women.

Reluctantly, Kara remained silent.

By the time they reached the wagon, Tony had gone inside. Kara found him sitting across his bunk with his gaze locked intently on the door as she walked in. Beside him sat her rucksack, packed full.

"I want you to go," he said before the door even closed behind her.

"Now?!"

Tony swallowed hard and held out her bag.

"Is this because of the boxers? Or because of what happened to the Wyatts?" she confronted him. "Do the Romani even have divorce? Is that what this is? Because you have really crappy timing to pull this after *midnight* on a night when there has been an attack, and *no one* is likely to open their doors if I knock."

A very un-Romani curse filled the wagon.

For a long moment, neither of them said anything. Kara reached out and took her bag from him, barely resisting the urge to snatch it from his grip. His eyes closed, squeezing tight as if to see her pained him. As if he expected she was going to walk out as he'd requested, and he couldn't bear to watch.

He had a long wait.

"Good night," she murmured as she headed for her cubby. Once behind her curtain, Kara stowed her bag and shucked her skirt before sliding back into bed. She lay there silently listening, half-expecting Tony to leave, but, after several long moments, he climbed under his sheets and thumped down on his bunk, clearly frustrated.

Chapter Four

Men from the nearby town came early the next morning to deal with the body. Strangers. Non-Romani. *Gorgio*, like her. They asked no questions and said not a word, despite the condition of the body. While they worked, the camp remained silent. No one ate a thing, though Kara saw plenty of coffee and harder drinks passed around. The strangers washed Robert Wyatts and dressed him in what seemed to be his best clothes, then stoppered his nose with wax and loaded him into a pine box waiting on the wagon they brought with them. Anything he owned of any value was piled around him, while the things that wouldn't bring even a copper were thrown right on to a waiting fire.

Once the wagon was loaded, a loud cry went up from every man, woman, and child of the clan. They cried and wailed and beat at their breasts as they followed the wagon on foot to the outskirts of the town. The women and children were clothed all in red or white, while the men wore black suits with white armbands. If not for their outcries, they would have resembled a parade.

Out of respect, and because she'd genuinely liked Robert, Kara joined them as they marched to where a stone church stood surrounded by tombstones; some bright white marble and crisp-edged, others worn until nary a word could be read beneath the blanketing moss. On the fringe of the cemetery was a fresh-dug grave with a simple wooden cross as a marker.

Once the pine box was lowered into the ground, each person there cast a single flower into the hole and went away, still wailing. The wagon holding the goods likewise pulled away, just after the strangers counted out a shockingly low number of bills onto Markos's palm. As they drove away, the clan leader tucked the money in Megan Wyatts' pocket. The woman barely seemed to notice as tears streaked down her face and vengeance smoldered in her gaze while she watched her brother interred. Never once did she cease in her wailing.

As the clan made the long march back, Kara noticed two heavy plumes of smoke hanging over the area where they had camped, but no one around her seemed surprised. The air grew acrid as they drew closer to the clearing. Trapped amid the mournful wailing, Kara barely heard the roar and crackle of the Wyatts' burning vardo, which swallowed up the pyre upon which many of Robert's worldly possessions had earlier been cast. Kara frowned at all of the destruction.

"But...what about Megan? Where..." she said as she turned to La-La, who plodded mutely beside her, only to fall silent at the disturbing look on her friend's face. A look between hunger and hatred glimmered deep in the woman's dulled eyes, or so it seemed in the brief second they held each other's gaze. Kara had to wonder if she'd imagined it, but she could have sworn she heard a hiss as La-La looked away.

From the other side of Kara, Tony spoke the first words he'd exchanged with her since their fight the previous night.

"It is considered bad luck...*Prikàza*...to keep the belongings of the deceased," he murmured. "It's like leaving their spirit an open invitation to come back, to exact retribution for any slight they may have felt was shown them when they were alive."

Kara just stared at him, dumbfounded. "*Seriously?*"

She remembered Sveta saying something similar, when Kara had first joined the caravan. It hadn't made sense then either.

He frowned back, glaring as his gaze darted to those around them.

Grimacing, she fell silent. Kara just couldn't understand. They had so little as it was. What sense did it make to burn all of Robert's perfectly good belongings when they surely could be used by *someone*? Then the memory rose of Susan Simko throwing away not just a perfectly good meal but also the pot it had been in, simply because Kara had taken a portion to feed Tony. A little guiltily, Kara also remembered whose soul—or a piece of it, anyway—resided in her violin. Who was she to question the Romani beliefs, even if she didn't hold them herself?

She sighed and shook her head as she watched Megan pick up what must have been a satchel of personal belongings and climbed into Sveta's wagon moving in odd jerky motions.

What was it La-La had said after the townies had attacked the camp...? *There is no point trying to make sense of the senseless.*

So close. So very close. The *Bás* fought the urge to lash out. Every instinct drove her to the kill, but too many surrounded them. She watched, her lip quivering as she drew in that sickly scent which for generations had steeped her race's hate. She grumbled and hissed beneath her host's breath. It was the same, and it was not the same. She scented the cursed one called Anu, but she also scented another; the spoor of ancient prey mingled with that of more recent prey as if one wore the other's skin as the *Bás* did her host. *Both* were known to her. Both were enemy. Both were...both were....*the same!*

The urge to strike nearly won. The *Bás* chittered and twitched within. She turned away lest she betray her hand too soon.

So close. So very close. Not close enough.

Yet.

They had left the last camp right after the funeral. It had been a long day of travel through unnatural heat, with Tony at the reins and Kara trapped inside, because it seemed most prudent. Their travel was done for now, and they had set up a new camp somewhere in the English countryside. Someplace called Cornrow...or Corn Hall or something like that.... Kara couldn't really say. She'd been so shocked Markos had bothered to tell her where they were going that she hadn't paid nearly as close attention as she should have.

Kara had just finished helping to set things to order after the evening meal and was ready to call it a night. When she entered the wagon, she found Tony stretched out on his bunk, his eyes dry but red, and his taut jaw white with tension. It had been a rough few days on all of them. She lowered her gaze and started to move past to her cubby.

"Why won't you stop haunting me?" Tony asked as she slipped by, his voice raw.

She stopped and looked back at him.

"I made a promise to Grandame Rose," Kara answered. "I haven't kept that promise yet."

He cursed and sent her a scathing look. "Do you see a bat-shit crazy demigod staring out of my eyes? The only thing I haven't been freed from is you." His gaze darted pointedly toward the door.

Kara crossed her arms and switched directions to sit at the built-in bench across from Tony's bunk, just as pointedly ignoring his less-than-subtle implication. A part of her wanted to be contrary and point out that Olcas had never stared out of his eyes; Olcas's eyes had stared out of his face. She restrained herself, but she did not allow herself to back down at Tony's aggression. Though she loathed acting merciless, she could not give in on this. If she did, she feared he would push her out for good and she would lose all chance to help him recover. He had been improving, but with everything that had happened with the deaths and the attacks, his inner demons had taken hold so tight it would not take much more to make him shatter. Kara could not let that happen. She knew what it was to be that broken, to have her soul hide from the world until all around her feared she would never return to them. Without Danu, Kara would have been lost within herself forever, consumed by the evil she had sought to hide from.

The scars from that time still marked her—beneath the flesh, if not upon it—but she had defeated her demons...*Tony's* demons both figuratively and literally. Maybe that was the problem. The 'bat-shit crazy' demigod Olcas and his brothers had been destroyed. Tony hadn't gotten to face them down himself. That didn't help Tony. He still struggled with the memories every day.

"Who do you see when you look in the mirror?"

"Back off!"

Anger. Frustration. Guilt. Despair. Tangible, almost crippling.

Kara braced herself against the maelstrom. "Who do you see?"

"Me!"

She hadn't expected that.

"Don't you get it?" he snarled as he sat up and swung his legs out of the bunk, leaning across the way to snap at her. "That's the problem. This isn't about *him*. It was never about him. I don't feel guilty because he used my body...I feel guilty because I couldn't *stop* him! Because once he knew that, he made me *watch*. Made sure I was aware and felt every damn thing HE did!

"I wasn't strong enough. I can never change that. I can never make up for it. Hell, I can barely live with it."

Kara held herself still as Tony pushed himself to his feet. Even with his height, he managed to pace the confines of the wagon. Kara resisted the impulse to jump when he smacked his hand against the far wall. He gripped the framework until the wood creaked.

"Every time you have a nightmare, or tell me something, or some other calamity hits I feel powerless again." As Tony spoke, his words grew softer, and he leaned his head against the wall. Tension stiffened his back, but all Kara could see was his sense of defeat. "What if that was you today..." he whispered, his voice cracking at the end. "That's all I keep thinking."

Slowly, carefully, she crossed the wagon to him. He arched and went rigid all over when she reached out and laid a gentle hand on his shoulder. He recoiled, whirling away and pressing his back against the wagon wall. Kara wanted to cry at his haunted expression.

"I'm sorry. I am so sorry," she murmured. "I was so certain I knew what you needed...how to help you. I never meant to make it worse."

"Self-absorbed much?" he snapped. "Not everything's about you."

Tony closed his eyes as if to shut out her hurt expression. He swallowed hard then he grimaced and shook his head sharply.

"You have helped me, but sometimes you push too hard. I'm not you. Sometimes what you say piles on my chest, like one rock after another, and I can't say a word. I can barely breathe. And then…then I can't even protect you."

Something fleeting flashed across his face, and he clenched his teeth harder. Kara frowned.

"What? What is it?"

"I think of what you've been through…what you've done…"

The muscles beneath her hand began to twitch, and Kara slowly drew away. Patiently, she waited, seeing the effort he made to say what he needed to say. Kara drew a sharp breath as Tony opened his eyes and she saw the anguish there. The words, when they came, were barely a whisper. A mere breath of air escaping between his teeth.

"I see how strong you are, and I feel ashamed." His voice dropped even lower until she could barely be sure she heard him speak at all. "I've lost everyone who's ever mattered. I'm afraid I'll lose you, too…and, just like all the others, there won't be a damn thing I can do about it."

She did not say a word. There was nothing she could say. Moving in slow, careful motions, she stepped forward and slid her arms around him. Briefly, he resisted, but there was nowhere for him to go without going through her. As he realized this, she felt him stiffen even further, then abruptly relax into her hold. He clutched her to him and folded himself around her, his whole body shaking with silent tears.

"You are strong, *so* strong," Kara murmured gently as her hair grew damp, and the tension slowly leached out of him. "Otherwise, you wouldn't still be here."

As night fell and most of the camp gathered around the communal fire, Kara sat on the steps of their wagon, her thoughts too turbulent for a social gathering, however informal. Tony had cried himself out but was clearly uncomfortable feeling so vulnerable and exposed. He'd asked her to give him some space. She'd gladly complied, but left Beag Scath behind to watch over him. Only now where was she to go?

"Why do you bait him?" a voice asked out of the darkness.

Kara took a moment to orient herself before responding. Unfurling her other senses, those ancient and magical, she placed her challenger and addressed him directly, eyes locking on where he stood with the ease she would have in daylight. With his swarthy skin and thick dark curls, the Rom had blended into the shadows, despite his height and bulk, lean but well-muscled. She was surprised to see him, though she didn't let on.

"I don't bait, Jacko. I don't pander either. He won't heal if he won't face the memories. Hidden wounds fester and rot. Scars that thicken unchecked are a prison for the soul."

The Rom smiled a sad, knowing smile and nodded his head in concession.

"What are you doing here?" Kara asked.

The last she knew, the man had set down roots somewhere in England with his wife, Agnieszka, the only *Sidhe* Kara knew of who refused to act like one.

He looked up at her, arching one thick, heavy brow. "You have no clue where you are, do you?"

Kara blushed. Other than knowing they were in Great Britain, she did not. One day on the caravan blended into another. Geography had never been her strong suit, outside of the boroughs of New York, anyway. As a native, she could navigate those blindfolded.

Jacko grinned, not unkindly, and leaned down to scoop something from the ground. When he straightened, he held a windfall apple. "Pitch this behind me with any force, and you'd like as not crack one of our windows. You're not just in Cornhill, you're camped on Wicklow land."

Corn*hill!* That was what Markos had told her.

The places Jacko mentioned echoed memories. Aí—a close friend among the *Tuatha de Danaan*, though not as close as he would like—had once shared with Kara the story of when he had been tasked with returning the hidden ones...the *Cosaints*...to the *Sidhe* lands. Agnieszka had been one of those *Sidhe* hidden to safeguard their race from extinction, and her home, Wicklow Cottage, was in Cornhill, England.

Kara drew a sharp breath and glanced back over at the gathered Rom, chatting away in their native tongue. Their laughter rose like bright embers borne upward on the fire's smoke and several among them tuned instruments. She recognized Larry Nelson and Patti Kinlock and another woman she knew only as Lowies, but the others were still vaguely familiar strangers to her. She was reminded that no matter how they had accepted her among them, she was an outsider...

She felt her shoulders lift as she breathed a sigh.

Jacko's gentle touch surprised her as his fingertips barely came to rest on her arm. "Come, *mora*...my friend," he told her. "We've fresh cider mulling on the stove, and I would love to hear of your journey with my clan thus far."

His words teased her tongue with the memory of the sharp-spiced bite of tart apples. She would have stepped forward to follow him only another memory rose up, this one bitter. The last Kara had seen the woman, Agnieszka had not been best pleased with anything *Sidhe*...or *Sidhe*-touched, her words biting and her ire fully raised. Time had passed, perhaps softening the woman's opinion, but Kara was something much more altogether with her human body and *Sidhe* soul. A stark reminder, one would think, of Agnieszka's lonely existence living a mortal life with no idea of her immortal nature.

Jacko must have sensed Kara's indecision. "No worries, *camlo*,"—lovely one—"She sent us to fetch you." At his words, a gentle weight pressed against Kara's leg. Glancing down, she spied a sweet, familiar face—human in appearance except for the diminutive proportions. Rex, one of the faeling. His presence reinforced Jacko's reassurance.

A smile broke Kara's indecision as she knelt to greet the sprite, the chosen friend and guardian of Agnieszka. The solemn, dusky sprite had latched upon the *Sidhe* woman as his special person with a fierceness that transcended his devotion to anyone else except Kara. His attitude toward her—as with all the faelings—was one of total adoration, but with a timid, hopeful air absent from her dealings with the others of his kind, as if he were uncertain of his reception. She had never been able to figure out why.

Kara held out her arms in invitation. *Chirling* much as a cat would, Rex clambered up her bent knee to enter her embrace. As Kara rose, Rex assumed the feline seeming favored by many sprites, his markings those of a dark, bold tabby stripe. He curled into the crook of her arm and purred.

"Well, that's decided, then, isn't it?" Jacko said as he turned to make his way through the night-darkened orchard edging the clearing where the caravan had set up camp. For a moment she considered returning to the wagon to grab Quicksilver; but Tony had asked for space, and Jacko had already disappeared from sight. She caught her lip between her teeth, torn about what to do.

"The cider's not going to drink itself," Jacko called out of the darkness. "But if you don't hurry, you might miss out on your share."

Kara laughed and hurried to catch up, her cheek resting against the faeling's soft warm forehead, allowing his rumbling purr to soothe her as she left behind the subtle tension of the Rom camp. That reminded her of something that had been bothering her for some time. A slight frown puckered her brow as she came up beside Jacko.

"Why aren't there any cats?"

He cocked his head a moment as if not following her.

She waved back toward the Romani camp. "No cats. Anywhere. Barely even any dogs...why?"

Jacko winced slightly as if uncomfortable before beckoning her to keep walking. She waited patiently for him to answer. They were halfway to the house before he spoke, the darkness swaddling them like a soft down comforter.

"There are no cats," he said, "because they are unclean. They touch the ground and lay on the ground. They roll around in the dirt and scratch in it to do their business. They eat rodents and other creatures of the dirt. The Romani believe to touch anything dirty is to become impure yourself, which opens you to illness and other misfortune."

Kara almost laughed. Cats? The most fastidious creatures on the face of the planet...*dirty*? She shook her head in disbelief. Again, it was like the situation with Susan Simko's pot or Robert Wyatts' belongings.

Kara frowned, her thoughts suddenly somber once more. It grew more evident to her that as much as she respected the Kalderaš Clan and loved living among them, she would *never* fit in. It wasn't just about learning the plethora of rigid social guidelines, there was a fundamental mindset that Kara could not hope to fully grasp. The Romani depended on compliance with that mindset for their very survival. Their beliefs had seen them through millennia of persecution and wandering that persisted to this day. With each new reminder of the differences between them, it became clear to Kara that she needed to decide where life would take her next because, as convenient as the travel was and as good the company, this was not a forever place for her.

"Hey, hey!" Jacko said, his tone jovial as he jostled her shoulder. "Come now, this is the time to visit with friends, not wax philosophical. For the moment, we are carefree, no?"

Kara laughed as he gamboled in the dark to break her from her solemn mood, tumbling and flipping with grace and skill, despite the near absence of light.

"That's what I like to hear!"

Not even breathing heavy, Jacko briefly threw his arm around her shoulders as they continued to the house. It was a friendly gesture, comforting. She relaxed and allowed herself to enjoy it. Even so, a thread of unease coiled around her heart as the motion reminded her of the absence of Quicksilver across her back.

The *Bás* watched from the dark, eyes narrowed and muscles taut and ready. The one that was both Anu and not Anu moved off with the one not-prey. With her gone, Danu, the Cursed One of all cursed ones, lay unguarded.

The *Bás* would soon deal with her ancient enemy.

And then...then she would move on to new prey.

For the first time in what seemed like forever, Tony was alone. He woke to near silence. No one hovering. No one casting worried glances or suspicious glares. No one in his head or in his space. Mostly that was just fine with him. Mostly.

The only sound was a faint scratching on the outside of the wagon. A branch, perhaps, or a bit of broken molding…it only served to remind him of the quiet surrounding him. The wagon had an empty air without Kara around. His *life* had an empty air without Kara around. He had to figure out which was worse: the constant reminder of how weak he had been and how others had suffered for it; or this hollow, panicked feeling that Kara wasn't returning.

Tony rolled over in his bunk and stared down the length of the wagon toward her space. The curtain was drawn back, and her bedclothes lay scattered over the pillow. His eyes darted away, noticing for the first time the little touches Kara had made around the wagon. A small vase of wildflowers on the table. A rag rug she had woven—with La-La's help—spread out on the floor. The outside of the wagon might still be rough and unkempt, but inside looked clean and homey.

He stood and wandered toward her space. Her gentle, earthy scent rose from the bedding, or maybe it was her little faerie friend he smelled. Tony could see the little guy peering out of the cabinet where Kara stored Quicksilver.

"How's it hanging, Beag Scath?" Tony nudged the door open further so he could see the wee one. He frowned when he saw the violin in its usual place. Kara rarely, if ever, left the wagon without Quicksilver.

Beag Scath grumbled and narrowed his eyes against the light, wrapping himself more firmly around the violin case.

Still frowning, Tony returned the cabinet to its nearly closed position and went to the wagon door. Outside, he could hear the muffled sounds of laughter and music. The clan had gathered around the communal fire. He'd likely find Kara among them. Or so he hoped. Still, he hesitated. At this point, none would question if he joined the circle, but, even before everything he had been through, he hadn't felt a proper part of the Romani community. He had the blood but not quite the proper upbringing.

There were times Kara fit in better than he did.

And then there were times she decidedly did not.

Tony grinned at the thought, his mood lightening a moment before worry took hold once more. Yes, he had asked her for some space, but an overwhelming need to find her gripped him now. Carefully, he pushed the door open, hoping Kara sat on the steps, as she often did, but he encountered no resistance as the door swung outward. He stood in the opening, peering into the night. The air was crisp and pleasantly smoky. The fire danced bright and hot in the center of the camp, intensifying the surrounding darkness. The clan gathered around it, eating and relaxing a bit before going to their rest. Some readied instruments, while others set theirs aside.

He was about to descend the steps when La-La appeared before him. Her gaze burned as bright as the fire behind her and tension had robbed her features of their customary softness.

"What's up?" he asked, his own tension creeping higher.

"Kara."

"She's not here, you'll—"

Before he could finish La-La tried to push past him.

"Hey!"

She snarled, and Tony backed away until he found himself beside Kara's bunk.

"What da hell, La-La?"

In silent sinuous motions, the woman padded forward. As she did, Tony blinked hard.

At first, La-La glowed. Then she changed. As she drew closer, it looked as if her spirit rose to the surface. Slowly it peeled away until La-La's body slumped to the floor, and what was left standing looked nothing like her.

"La-La!" Tony nearly hurried forward before he realized what happened. He choked as a pungent musk filled the wagon.

One of the *Namhaid* stalked toward him, claws distended and her gaze predatory. A deep crimson tongue flicked out between deceptively delicate fangs as the spirit woman eyed him like a feast.

Tony glared back, baring his teeth. There was nowhere to evade the creature in the tight space of the wagon. He spread his stance and drew on the memories of his time bound by Olcas. With his mage power, he first anchored to the earth and raised a shield against the beast before him, then he gathered energy, ready to lash out.

She ignored him as she turned and reached for the cabinet housing Quicksilver.

"No *fuckin'* way," Tony said with a snarl of his own. He lunged forward and snatched the violin away, holding it—and Beag Scath, who still clung to it—high and behind him. At the same time, he slammed the *Namhaid* with a mage bolt.

She shimmied as if in ecstasy then smirked at him as she absorbed the power.

"You will make a fine crèche for my young."

Then she pounced. With one taloned hand, she gripped his throat. With the other, she lashed out at Quicksilver. Tony barely noticed the jolt as she connected with the instrument. He was too focused on what was happening to him.

Wherever the *Namhaid* touched him tendrils of her essence bound with his.

Oh, *hell* no! Not again...

"Find Kara!" Tony yelled to the sprite, then he fought off the *Namhaid* with everything he'd ever learned from the bat-shit-crazy demigod's example.

Chapter Five

"Watch where you're stepping, now!" a prim, proper, and slightly annoyed British voice called from the doorway as Kara and Jacko approached the back door of the cottage. Backlit as she was, Agnieszka Anne Michaels' white hair glowed like a halo, while her silhouette was slender of limb, youthful, and undeniably gravid. She stood with one hand gripping the doorjamb, and the other braced at her lower back. "I just got the damned garden replanted!"

Kara stumbled as Agnieszka's words reminded her of the things Aí had told her, and why the garden had needed replanting to begin with. This was one of the places the *Namhaid* had struck before the Battle of the Knock, when Agnieszka was still *Cosaint* and ignorant of her own nature; the woman had nearly been one of their victims. Kara needed to warn her...

Blissfully unaware, Jacko simply laughed and made an exaggerated show of wending a careful path across the yard, beckoning Kara to follow precisely in his footsteps. At the sound of the woman's answering chuckle, Rex pulled away from the cradle of Kara's arms and leaped away, appearing within seconds at the woman's feet.

Agnieszka. A *Sidhe* woman who'd grown up believing herself human. The last Kara had seen her was in *Tir na nÓg* at the Welcoming, a ritual that cleansed *Sidhe* souls of the memories of their past life in preparation for being reborn. Other than that one concession, the woman eschewed all things to do with the *Tuatha de Danaan.*

By human reckoning, Agnieszka was sixty years old, approaching her golden years. By *Sidhe* reckoning, she was barely of consenting age. She was also the only person Kara knew of who had ever put Goibhniu in his place. Even now, Agnieszka refused to give up her quiet human life, a life built on heartache and deception, but decidedly her own. Frankly, Kara was astounded she'd been invited for a visit, given her own unique relationship with the *Tuatha de Danaan.* Her situation oddly echoing Agnieszka's, having been born human, only to discover she was *Sidhe.*

"Well? Are you coming in or not?"

Kara jumped as the impatience in Agnieszka's voice.

"Sorry," she murmured as she joined Jacko on the stoop. "Thank you for the invitation to visit."

"*Hmph.* Come on then, the cider won't drink itself."

Kara nearly laughed at Agnieszka's almost verbatim repetition of Jacko's earlier comment, but she thought better of it. Instead, she looked around as she followed the couple through a neat, pleasant kitchen into an equally homey parlor filled with the rich earthy warmth of a peat fire, part of her still trying to figure out how to warn them about the *Namhaid.*

"Sit." Agnieszka motioned them both to the sofa and gently worn mix-matched chairs arranged around the cozy fire. "I'll be right back."

"Ah! No...no, you sit, little mother," Jacko said, practically picking Agnieszka up and plopping her in the chair closest to the warm stone hearth.

Though her lips were pursed, there was no denying the love and wonder in Agnieszka's gaze as her husband hurried out to the kitchen. Kara almost felt she was intruding.

"Infuriating man," Agnieszka murmured. "Do you know, he's always called me that, even before..."—and here the woman grimaced—"Before I was the size of a cow."

"Oh tosh," Jacko scoffed as he came back in with a tray of steaming mugs, the intoxicating aroma of warm apple and spices preceding him. It almost sounded as if he mimicked her. "You're barely the size of a sheep!"

She glared at him, but there was no anger to it.

He laughed joyously, and Kara joined him, noticing the same wonder lurking in his expression as if neither he nor Agnieszka dared to quite believe they'd attained their hearts' desire. After handing Kara her mug, Jacko folded himself to the ground beside his wife's chair, his head leaning against her knee.

With her words full of mirth, Kara quipped, "Maybe I should take this to go..."

Agnieszka blushed, muttering a prim "Nonsense."

Each of them settled in comfortable silence, carefully sipping their hot beverages. Kara was reminded of similar nights with her parents, only with mugs full of rich cocoa. She breathed a relaxed sigh and allowed herself to savor the moment. This place was a haven of peace in the midst of the recent turmoil.

As if sensing her thoughts, Jacko sat forward, his expression solemn and his gaze shadowed. "Tell me, how is my cousin?"

Kara's brow twisted in confusion. She knew Jacko was of the Kalderaš Clan. In fact, he was Sveta's brother, but she hadn't a clue who he meant when he said 'cousin'. To be truthful, she didn't understand the family dynamics of the Romani any better than she did their beliefs.

"Tony, *chey*."—*girl*—"How is Tony?"

"Oh!"

She felt a bit dim not to have realized right away. Who else would Jacko ask her about?

A halfhearted smile lifted one corner of her lips. "He's doing okay. Much better than he was. He's started coming out of himself, taking an active part in the clan. There are rough patches, but he's making progress."

"Ah! Good, good!"

Good. But not good. Kara had no excuse now, no call to put off the conversation any longer.

"There's something else though..." She frowned and took a long drink from her mug, loath to break the peace of the moment. But she already had, hadn't she? Both Jacko and Agnieszka tensed, their gazes locked on her and their cider forgotten.

Grimacing, Kara opened her mouth to explain only to be interrupted as a sharp bang sounded from the kitchen, as if the back door had been flung open. She set down her mug and jumped up only slightly faster than Jacko. Agnieszka beat them both to their feet. Before any of them moved any further, Rex and Beag Scath darted into the room.

The only word Kara could think of to describe their behavior was 'furious'. They transformed from cat to pixie in dizzying flashes, and, even as she watched, Beag Scath drew great ropes of mage power from the landscape around them, growing physically large with each grab as if preparing for battle. He pinned her with a gaze most urgent and uttered one word: "Namhaid!"

Kara had just enough time to hear Agnieszka and Jacko gasp before Beag Scath grabbed her hand and whisked her away through the void.

It was happening again.

Evil was about to triumph, and Tony DeLocosta wasn't strong enough to do anything about it.

Once again Kara O'Keefe would suffer because he was too weak.

Nothing he tried worked. He pushed the Namhaid back, she stayed pushed only as long as it took to suck up whatever energy he threw at her. He shielded; he dodged; he took the blows just trying to get close enough to shut the bitch down. All he'd managed to do is wear himself out and spill his own blood. The Namhaid? She laughed at him as she licked it off her claws.

Despair nearly zapped what strength Tony had left. He gritted his teeth and shoved it away.

He stopped attacking and raised a shield once more, determined to stand between the creature and Quicksilver, ready to spend his last breath to ensure Kara didn't lose another piece of herself because of him. He watched his adversary stalk forward with the deadly grace of a panther.

Self-doubt whispered in his ear, telling him he was the mouse.

She toyed with him. Just like Olcas had.

No. No! He clenched his jaw and bared his teeth. *Not again! Never again!*

Tony took a deep breath and considered what he'd tried so far.

Great sweeping blasts of power tossed about without much thought or strategy, like anger-driven punches, formless and uncontrolled.

—fear-driven, his doubt taunted—

Time after time until he felt like nothing but a shadow of himself. A good way to fail. A good way to die.

Fight smarter, not harder, he thought to himself.

Tony drew more power, struggling not to sway as fatigue flooded him. He lashed out, then narrowed his gaze, watching what the *Namhaid* did.

As she siphoned the power, Tony was reminded of the way her spirit had tried to bond with his, kind of the way oxygen bonded with hydrogen to make water.... And wouldn't his chemistry teacher, Mr. Panek, fall over in shock if he knew Tony had pulled that memory out of nowhere.

Focus, Tony!

Where the hell had his mind been going with that?

The *Namhaid*...she was incomplete! Just like in chemistry, she filled in the gaps in her outer shell with whatever she could grab. Whether Tony's essence or that of the mage energy...

Big and powerful wouldn't do the trick. Tony needed tight and focused, with no loose bits to give the evil bitch something to latch on to.

In the back of his mind, he almost thought he heard a murmur of approval.

Again, the *Namhaid* lashed out, claws scraping down Tony's shield, shredding it and lapping up the pieces, proving his point.

Reaching deep down, Tony dredged up more power. Just a bit. First a little puff, blowing it out big and fluffy. While that distracted the *Namhaid*, Tony swiftly drew some more, eyes squeezing shut against the spots swimming before them.

Focus.

There wasn't much energy left. Tony could barely control it. But he had to. With everything he had, he visualized a thin, hard spear of power, smooth as glass, hard as titanium. Hard, and tight, and focused. Needle-like and precise. For just a moment, he held it perfect and complete, then he launched it at the enemy.

As he tumbled into darkness, all he heard was a piercing shriek, and he felt all the energy he had left go leaping away.

The Romani camp was in turmoil as Kara fell out of the void, struggling to keep her feet beneath her and the contents of her stomach where they belonged. Traveling the void was bad enough with warning, but absolutely brutal with none. She stumbled toward Tony's wagon with Beag Scath weaving about her feet in agitation. Something was wrong. The wagon...the mage energy it had been imbued with...it was gone. She tried to peer closer through the darkness. It looked like someone, or some*thing* had gouged the carvings, destroying the charms that protected those inside against evil.

The door hung open, but she could see nothing more for all the Rom hurrying past.

"Tony!" Kara called out, fighting the bile that surged up her throat.

She stopped abruptly as the way before her cleared.

Tony braced himself in the doorway his face pale and drained. Physically, angry red scratches circled his throat, trailing runnels of blood. They matched a half-dozen others on visible skin and who knew how many more beneath the slashes in his clothes. Her heart tightened at the sight of him, worried at the injuries, but joyous to see him breathing.

"Tony..." she repeated, this time barely a whisper.

He looked up and met her eye. She swayed at the strength she saw in his expression. The crippling doubt, the shame, the self-recrimination...all the demons Tony had fought for months, she saw none of them reflected in his gaze. Were they merely subdued, or banished? Whichever proved true, for now, he exuded an aura of serenity.

"You're okay," Kara said.

Tony nodded. "I'm okay."

"The *Namhaid*?"

Tony's jaw clenched. "Not dealt with, but fought off."

Kara nodded. "I'll take gone for now, any day, over the other possibilities," she said with relief, remembering the carnage when the *Namhaid* had attacked *Tir na nÓg*. While clearly Tony and others in the camp had not gone unscathed, Kara was relieved she hadn't come back to worse.

At her words, Tony dropped his gaze, but she had already seen the turmoil there.

"What?"

"The *Namhaid* was after Quicksilver."

Kara felt the blood drain from her face. Without a word, she pushed passed him.

At some point, Beag Scath had darted inside without her notice. Once more his normal size, the sprite huddled by her bunk, keening. Gently, Kara moved him aside, lifting him to shelter beneath her hair.

She felt more than heard as Tony came up behind her, but all of her attention was focused on the violin. With hands that trembled, she opened the ravaged case.

The bow lay in two pieces, the severed horsehairs splayed across the instrument, hiding Quicksilver from full view. Kara was afraid to move them.

"Is she okay?" Tony asked in hushed tones, the words barely a breath, as if he feared what her answer would be.

She just looked up at him, not knowing how to answer.

Anguish and fresh guilt filled his expression, but only briefly. She marveled as he subdued the negativity, instead of feeding it.

"The Lady…she sometimes spoke to me," Tony mumbled, not quite meeting Kara's gaze. "At night, when the darkness piled on top of me, or you cried out in your sleep, she would murmur. Nonsense mostly, I guess, until we both calmed down and settled, like a mom does."

He sounded just a bit unsure.

Vaguely, Kara remembered he had lost his parents young and been mostly raised by Granddame Rose. Then what he said sank in. Danu. *Danu* talked to him. As far as Kara knew, he was the only person other than her Grandda and herself that the goddess had made an effort to speak to. Few others even knew the spirit existed within the violin.

Kara turned her gaze back to Quicksilver.

She almost moaned at the damage as she drew the pieces of the bow away. The *Namhaid*'s claws had not just sliced through the case and bow, they'd cut the strings and gouged shallow furrows across Quicksilver's body. There weren't any cracks that Kara could see. But that was all surface. Physical. She was afraid to look deeper. To reach within. It terrified her to consider what she might find.

Or *not* find.

She shivered as numbing cold crept through her limbs.

Tony crouched beside her and pulled her close until she nestled against his chest. Kara's eyes drifted closed as Tony's heat enveloped her. For a moment, she let herself relax into his hold, laughing wearily as Beag Scath huffed in annoyance before fleeing his haven beneath her hair. Then she felt the pulse of Tony's heart against her shoulder, and her own slowed down to keep pace with it.

"Are *you* okay?"

Her heartbeat sped up again. Kara looked up into his face, astounded. He sounded as if that mattered even more than the violin. *How had things changed so quickly between them?*

"Danu," Kara murmured, gently tugging herself free. She felt ice cold as fears dodged around in her brain. "Her name is Danu. She is the sister of my soul, and mother goddess to the *Sidhe*. And a piece of her lived...*lives* inside my violin." On the last words, Kara's voice broke. Her fingers trembled as she reached out to caress the damaged wood. Even before she knew of her powers, the violin had held a place in her heart. Since then, both Quicksilver and Danu had become entwined with her until there was no clear line between any of them.

She held her breath as the barest tip of her finger brushed the belly. Then she sobbed and nearly collapsed on top of the instrument. Would have, if not for Tony's arms wrapping once more around her, keeping her from crushing Quicksilver to splinters and strings. She could hear Tony's relieved laugh beside her ear as both of them felt more than heard the grumbling murmurs of the goddess within.

Relief made Kara weak. "She's there. Oh, my God, she's there!"

"Well, a piece of her, anyway," Tony responded as he sat back against the base of the bench, drawing her with him.

Tony's words triggered a memory.

The sprite, T.Rob, all but chastising her. What had he said...?

"You're all put back together. Now it's her turn..."

Kara hadn't understood then, but he'd been talking about Danu!

She grabbed Quicksilver before Tony pulled her out of reach, stroking the violin's belly as Tony stroked hers, soothing and comforting, or trying to, anyway. His casual words, combined with the memory of T.Rob, shot straight to Kara's heart, unwittingly foiling Tony's efforts.

One piece. They had safeguarded *one piece.* How many more were scattered around the world? She had to find them....before the *Bás* did.

The urge to howl gripped her. Her form shook with the need to turn back and fight, but the fleeing one resisted. In the *Bás*, the drive for survival ran stronger than any other impulse.

She had the scent of her enemy. She had the knowledge of how to hide. She had the form of another host, snatched from among the not-prey as she fled.

This was not defeat. It was a strategic withdrawal.

The enemy *would* pay. Just not today.

The *Bás* were patient. They had been waiting for a very long time.

Kara watched as the Romani women led La-La away toward a nearby wagon. Part of Kara felt shame that she had not noticed her friend collapsed on the vardo floor in her rush to get to Quicksilver, but mostly she rejoiced that La-La still lived.

Kara longed to go with her, to help her, but she had learned her lesson with Tony. The Romani woman would need to find her own way of healing. With help, to be sure, but in her own time and at her own pace. Kara just prayed the clan had also learned, and La-La's path to recovery would not be as arduous as Tony's.

As the door to the vardo closed, Kara turned away only to come face to face with the leader of the Kalderaš Clan. She winced at the damage he'd taken when the *Namhaid* fled. His left cheek bore a deep, dark bruise that would take some time to go away, and the scratches cutting across it had been cleaned but remained raw and red. Kara saw resolution in his gaze, along with regret.

"We had trouble enough of our own just being Romani. Since you joined us that has trebled. You might not cause the trouble, but your very presence seems to lure it in." Markos grimaced, and his gaze flickered briefly away as if remorse poked at him. Without a doubt, Kara knew the words he regretted to say, had even anticipated them. "We are grateful and will always count you as close as kin, but you must go."

They hurt to hear just the same. With a sad smile, Kara stepped forward and kissed his undamaged cheek. "No worries. Never would I wish more hardship upon the clan. I have already accepted my path lies elsewhere."

Someone cleared their throat behind her.

"Our path."

Kara whipped around, her gaze widening as it met Tony's.

"*Our* path," he repeated.

Slowly, she nodded as she stepped toward him and took the hand he held out to her.

Bonus Stories

Bonus Stories Acknowledgments

"The Birth of Anu's Children" published in a previous version as
the Prelude to the novel, *Tomorrow's Memories*, published by both
Mundania Press and Dark Quest Books, respectively.

"Blessed by the Fae" published in a previous version as the Prelude to
the novel, *Today's Promise*, published by Dark Quest Books.

"The Promise of Death" published in a previous version in the
anthology *Were-*, Zombies Need Brains LLC.

"Forever and a Day" published in a previous version in the anthology
Fantastic Futures 13, Padwolf Publishing.

"Travellin' Show" published in a previous version in the anthology
Space Tramps, Flying Pen Press.

"The Devil's Own Luck" published in a previous version in the
anthology *Lucky 13*, Padwolf Publishing.

The Birth of Anu's Children

(Prelude to *Tomorrow's Memories*)

SHROUDING THEMSELVES WITH STARLIGHT AND MIST, TWO FIGURES sought to elude death's relentless pursuit. The faithful wind whipped behind them, blurring the signs of their passage, and in its newness, the moon betrayed them not.

Graceful even in their panic, Anu and Danu locked away their grief to fight for their survival. Anu stumbled, tangled by the tall, wind-plaited grass. Locks of shimmering red hair escaped from her travel braids. The tresses mingled with the grass, giving the illusion that Anu was being pulled under, consumed by the meadow.

Danu frantically reached back for the reassurance of her sister's hand. She could not allow Anu to fall behind. From the very womb their fingers had intertwined and if they were to leave this life, she wanted it to be in the same way.

As their hands clasped, Danu nearly faltered. Drawing her focus away from what stalked them, she settled her senses on her sister. Both love and determination filled Anu's brown eyes to brimming as they met hers. The pain and despair she saw there also nearly brought Danu down. Death did not follow in their footsteps; it ran in stride beside them.

"Do na do it, *Lhiannon*." *Sweetheart*. Anu gently but forcefully admonished her twin. "We'll be needin' our strength for the tasks before us—the worse for you an' ye make me waste one bit o' what I have left tryin' to comfort ye. Ye must away with ye an' na trouble yer heart over what canna be helped." As if to lend force to her words, she wrenched her hand free.

Danu trembled violently. She wanted to cry out, to deny the truth, but she could not. Her sister's end drew nearer with each step. Danu sensed more than saw the wound carrying her twin across the Veil. A horrible rent tore down Anu's side, her heart's blood brimming and seeping from it. A muted sparkle of power kept the blood from flowing freely, but as her sister's strength waned, the stream would gain force. Danu's grief held her silent. Anu was her strength...the completion of her heart.

"No! There is'na time for that. Now listen hard: ye must flee from here. Falias, Finias, an' Gorias are but scorched rubble, an' Murias...Murias has fallen into shadow, the gates forever closed to the *Daoine Maithé*." Anu cast a haunted glance the way they had come. Danu's gaze could not help but follow.

For the moment, she saw no sign of pursuit. The surface of the plain swayed beneath the stars in a deceptively peaceful air that clashed with Danu's memories of the carnage and destruction, of city streets painted crimson with blood, lit by the fiery glow of ancient homes turned to pyres. The ravaged remains of their people had been strewn about the cobbles in cruelly crumbled heaps, left to lie where they had fallen in their attempts to defend their kin and homes. The corpses were few, though no hope lay in this, for Anu's Sight had shown that the others had not fled to freedom; rather they had been rounded up like livestock to meet their fate at the convenience of the enemy. Only the sisters had escaped, traveling between cities at the time of the attack.

No doubt they would share the same doom if they were caught. Already the *Namhaid—the enemy—*were ruthless in their pursuit.

She drew her attention back to Anu's words, eerily echoing her thoughts. "Even now the *Namhaid Conairt* follow us, as sure as hounds, an' soon there will be more on our trail. They must'na find ye, they canna be allowed to drag ye down like the rest o' us or the *Daoine Maithé* will be dust forever."

Her good hand clutched painfully at Danu's shoulder for but an instant before her strength faltered.

"Ye do na understand, do ye?" Anu demanded. Her breath was thready and it was a moment before she continued. "Sorrow has blinded ye. 'Tis only for now ye'll stand alone, an ye survive the hunt, 'tis yerself that'll see that the *Daoine Maithé* rise up again." Anu's hand came to rest on Danu's smooth, flat belly. "I'll na be lost to ye forever, then. Now away with ye! I canna last much longer an' I've one more task to see to."

Danu clasped her sister to her, barely suppressing the keen that welled up in her throat. Without even a thought, she sent a stream of power across the link that bound them. Before her sister could block her, she rooted her soul with Anu's, deeper even than the constant bond they had shared since the womb. Danu shared every ounce of herself in that instant before Anu ripped herself away with a burst of love and regret.

"Ye wee fool, ye have'na strength to squander." Anu struggled a moment as her throat grew thick and tears pricked her eyes. "Now away with ye, an' let me do as I may to see ye safely free."

Anu waited until Danu was well away before luring the hunters to herself. Only when she could neither see nor sense her sister's fleeing form did Anu release the barest trickle of her own power, as good as a beacon in the night. Already the wind carried the snarls and shouts of their pursuers. She must muddle the trail that would betray her beloved sister before the *Conairt* descended upon her.

Tearing a bloody scrap from her tunic, Anu fought to keep her hand steady as she probed the open wound in her side. Her teeth clenched and sweat glistened on her brow as she ruthlessly grasped a sliver of bone from the wreckage of her ribs and snapped it free. Not even the rigid control acquired over centuries of life could hold back the scream of agony the act tore from her throat. Triumphant howls mockingly echoed her wail, chilling her to her core as they drew closer.

Damn! She would have to work quickly. Gathering all she could spare of her dwindling energy, Anu pulled her travel blade from its sheath and sawed furiously at the thinnest of her braids. Then, with careful haste, Anu wrapped the bone in a scrap she tore from her tunic and tied it fast with the severed strands. She held it in the now free-flowing stream of blood spilling from her side, all the while chanting fervently in the ancient tongue. Uncontrolled by her fevered mind, all manner of images began to form, fantastic creatures, both fair and foul, with jeweled wings and needle-like teeth, fey eyes and fickle manner, leviathans of the deep and wispy spirits; all that was darkness and light filled her thoughts, interwoven with her memories of joy and fear and grief. Her imagination formed legions of faery folk never before seen upon the earth. Their sole purpose: to confuse and distract the *Namhaid Conairt* with tantalizing whiffs of borrowed power, giving Danu time to flee.

Anu kept nothing back for herself; death already held her close. She raised the crude fetish to her face and blew upon it, guiding her creations with all the magic at her disposal. A mist sparkling with power enveloped Anu as she sank to her knees, arms raised above her head in entreaty. The vapors took on her imagined shapes until one by one she released her only children to the world, feeling a bit of her soul drain away with each one. In her mind, she whispered their names: púca, sprite, fairy, redcap, yeti, leprechaun, ki-lin, selkie, lamai, and so on until each of them knew themselves.

With what felt like her last breath, Anu crumbled to the ground. She could not even muster a sense of satisfaction, as she lay upon the flattened grasses, vaguely aware of the approaching sounds of her pursuers.

And then she saw them. Their red eyes glowed in the near-black night and their short white pelts shimmered like crushed velvet. Thick manes of fiery red hair whipped about their bare shoulders and breasts, while razor-like fangs gleamed almost daintily in their open mouths...open to allow their dragging breaths to taste the scent of the sisters on the air. Their own musk rose heavy and cloying, leaving Anu longing for one last breath of crisp, clean air. How could they possibly filter through enough of their own scent to track anything less potent than they?

She would never know.

They were upon her and she could not even gather the energy to cross the Veil by her own hand, rather than allow them the satisfaction of taking her. She just laid there, eyes raised to the stars, as they circled and baited. Vicious in their frustration, cheated by her passiveness, they sought to draw from her a more gratifying reaction; they lashed out with raking claws and taunted her with flicks of their rasping tongues as if she were a bit of candied fruit. They continued to howl their chilling cries. Moans and growls of battle-lust filled her ears and yet her only thought was to wonder where Danu would find herself when finally she stopped running.

And then she felt a sense of peace—a Vision danced before her, images of a strange, vast island of green, rolling hills and impressive granite cliffs surrounded by seas trimmed in white, lacy froth as they broke upon the rocky shore. Danu would thrive there among the ancient groves and moors, surrounded by her Clan of children.

Finally, her sister's face floated before her mind's eye. With her final breath, Anu muttered a curse at that beloved one. The name Danu was on her still lips as they dragged her away to Murias.

"Imeacht gan teacht ort, A chuisle mo chroí!" May you leave without returning. The words whispered on the wind at her back, but Danu knew her sister's love had turned that common curse into an anchor to help her remain steadfast in the time to come. May she leave without returning, indeed; Danu had no doubt that it would be a blessing to never see this cursed shore again. She shared her sister's mortal agony, felt the hand of death upon her own shoulder, but she'd also brought away with her the surety of hope. It was time to take that elsewhere and resurrect their people, to be the vessel through which their souls would once again enter the earth.

Putting the darkness from her mind, she focused on what her beloved twin had called her: *A chuisle mo chroí! O pulse of my heart!* The phrase was more usually shared between lovers, but in using it, Anu had given her a gift, for now Danu could not dwell on the heartache without knowing her wounded heart beat for both of them. Anu's sacrifice had secured a future for them all. Danu would find a new home; there to bear her children... and the *Daoine Maithé*—the Good People—would once again lift their faces to the sun and moon and wind.

Blessed by the Fae

(Prelude to *Today's Promise*)

THE HOPE AND DREAD ON BARBARA'S FACE WAS HEART-WRENCHING TO behold.

Conall O'Keefe entered the box-strewn kitchen looking for his wife. Instead, he found his daughter-in-law clutching the countertop on either side of the sink. Her thin cotton shirt clung to her, and she was as coated with dirt as the worn linoleum beneath her feet. Perhaps it was the moonlight streaming in the window, or perhaps merely the strain of a day much longer than any of them had anticipated, but poor Barbara looked paler than skimmed milk. A single teardrop mingled with the dirt and the sweat beaded upon her face.

"Oh, darlin', a bit much for ye, is it?" he asked softly. "Ready to call it a night?"

Her eyes drifted closed, and her head fell back. Conall did not miss the reflexive gulp that rippled across her outstretched throat. *Oh, damn!* Within seconds Barbara started trembling, and it occurred to Conall that what he'd happened upon was more than utter exhaustion.

"Paddy! Paddy, get yer arse in here!" Conall bellowed as he quickly crossed the room to Barbara's side. Before he reached her, she jerked with a growing spasm until she bent over the sink and heaved. The sickly sweet smell of bile drifted toward him and he hurried forward to catch his son's wife as her knees buckled, and she lost her grip on the Formica countertop.

"Sweet Lord! Patrick! Where are ye?! Moira?" He cradled Barbara against his chest with one arm and reached for the spigot with the other. As he opened the tap a spurt of rusty water poured from the rarely used pipes before the flow ran clear, rinsing the bile and sick down the drain.

Grabbing at the roll of paper towels on the counter he gave a quick, sharp jerk to tear off a sheet without the whole of it unwinding. Wetting it in the running water, he gently wiped off Barbara's face. He tossed the soiled towel aside and turned off the water, before he called out again, "Can I get a hand down here, or na? Barbara's ill."

He could hear the others hurry across the floor upstairs, apparently bumping into packing crates and stumbling over items already removed from the boxes. Satisfied they would be there in a moment, Conall peered around the kitchen. He needed to sit down, but cartons covered every surface, including the mismatched, straight-backed chairs he and Moira had given the children until they could get a kitchen set of their own. A glance in the open box on the closest chair confirmed that it held nothing more than kitchen towels and other linens. A quick shove with his foot and the box hit the floor, freeing up the seat. Conall nudged the chair around until he could settle into it without disturbing his daughter-in-law. He focused all his attention on Barbara, seating her more securely in his lap and pushing back the sweat-darkened blonde curls from her face. He did not miss the quick flutter of her eyes or her quavering breath, evidence she was conscious, though she remained limp in his arms. And then he noticed something else more disturbing.

"Come now, Bobbi-lass, look at me," he murmured gently. "How long have ye been hidin' this?"

Tears streamed from beneath her lowered eyelids and her delicate hand came up to clutch the front of his green cardigan as she buried her face against his shoulder. He heard a gasp from the across the room. A moment later, his son knelt beside him, panic glistening in his deep brown eyes. Conall's wife, Moira, stood quietly in the doorway, her sturdy frame leaning against the jamb out of necessity, as there was no more room in the kitchen. Something in her gaze told him that she already suspected what he had just discovered: Barbara was again with child.

The hope and dread now made complete sense.

Barbara O'Keefe hunched on her own chair at the care-worn table, trying to pretend that three sets of eyes weren't riveted on her. She didn't like being the center of such intense scrutiny. This was why she had kept her suspicions to herself. The heartache was bad enough, endured so many times before, without their fears amplifying her own.

This was not her first pregnancy; it was her fourth. In two years...and she had yet to give Patrick O'Keefe a child. Each of her previous pregnancies had been difficult, all ending in miscarriages. She was not supposed to have gotten pregnant again so soon...if ever, at all. Dr. Cohen cautioned that another miscarriage might kill her.

"Why, Bobbi?" her husband spoke in hushed, fearful tones. "Why did ye na take the wee pills the doctor gave ye?"

Why indeed? She was not so good a Catholic that the Church's prohibition against birth control caused an issue for her. That element of matters had been more of an issue for Patrick himself. Then the doctor had outlined the risks of another pregnancy. Her husband's objections had quickly fallen away.

The medication was not a problem. In fact, in the short time she had taken it, she experienced none of the adverse side effects her doctor warned were possible. No, she had simply woken one day and reached for her packet, only to find herself overwhelmed by a sensation of wrongness and frustration. A sensation that she stood in the way of something meant to be. From that point forward, she could not bring herself to take the pills. But she had not been able to confess so to her husband.

"I don't know," she whispered. Guilt crept over her and she could not look any of them in the eye.

"Ye don' know? Ye don' know!?" Patrick's voice cracked, and Barbara could feel fresh tears slide down her cheeks. He was frightened, not angry, and that alone kept her from breaking down completely. Her in-laws said nothing, though she knew they too questioned the wisdom of her actions.

"I'm sorry," she said. "I'm so sorry..." No other words would come and these were less than adequate. Her gaze darted up to look into Patrick's face. He was barely twenty-four. Right now he looked at least ten years older, his face gaunt with worry and his eyes burning with fear.

What had she done?

Conall woke to the familiar sound of retching coming from the bathroom down the hall. His heart went out to his daughter-in-law as he lay beside his wife staring at the still-unfamiliar walls of their room. They had not intended to move into their son's new home, but given Barbara's unexpected condition, all had agreed it would be for the best. Two months had passed since that fateful night of discovery. It had not been easy on any of them since. The elder O'Keefes helped their son shoulder the burden of settling in and running the new household, but Barbara grew increasingly wan, and her morning sickness lasted nearly all day.

Conall suspected that, by this point, tension and fear more than anything else caused Barbara's rough term, but they were long past the time of reassuring words. The first failed pregnancy had been taken in stride, but by the second miscarriage, late in the fifth month, the sense of doom had begun to take hold. The third pregnancy had not gone for even two months. Now they all fought to hold onto hope.

"We hardly need bother with an alarm, now, do we?" Conall's harmless jest earned him a smack from his still-sleepy wife. He knew the comment had been in poor taste, but he scarcely knew how else to vent his frustration, other than the occasional snarky remark. There was no doubt their presence made a significant difference but was it enough? The fear of losing another grandchild was pure, protracted hell; yet it was nothing compared to the torment faced by Patrick and Barbara. What Conall wouldn't give to magically make things right...but no...he had already made a trip down to Yesterday's Dreams, the pawn-shop owned by Maggie McCormick, only to be told there was nothing more she could do. Even had her skill lay within the realm of healing, which it did not, every bit of magic they had tried to safeguard the two previous pregnancies had failed. No, there would be no instant fix; only their prayers and diligence could make a difference now.

Again, the sound of retching and Conall glanced over at the little travel clock across the room; Patrick was long gone on his way to work. It was time for them to offer what comfort they could.

He looked at Moira. "Ye know I don't mean a thing by it. Hand me the crackers an' I'll go see to her."

Barbara heard Conall humming in the hallway, the sound joyous and lively. It woke her to a hunger she hadn't realized was there. He used to bring out his violin nightly, but for months they had all been too tired for such things. She missed it fiercely.

"Da?" Even to her own ears, the call was weak.

Patrick's father leaned into the doorway, his expression kind and patient, his arms filled with a basket of her dirty laundry that he must be carrying downstairs for Mathair. Barbara was overcome with guilt. At a time when they should be planning retirement cruises and shopping for that sailboat they had always wanted, her in-laws were instead taking over all the duties she no longer had the energy to do. He and Mathair O'Keefe were working so hard because she had selfishly allowed herself to get pregnant. And now she would add to this loving man's burden, and for what? Because she was music-starved and lonely...

"What is it, Bobbi-lass?"

She wanted to tell him never mind...that she was sorry to have interrupted, but she couldn't. Tears made her eyes glisten as she pressed her lips tightly closed against one of the uncontrollable emotional tempests that tore at her with increasing frequency.

Conall made soothing sounds and set his basket down, moving to sit beside her on the edge of the bed. With a gentle touch, he wiped away an escaped teardrop. "Come now...ye've had yer shower already, have ye na?"

Barbara laughed and twined her fingers with his as he reached down and took up her hand. She gave a little squeeze and leaned against his shoulder. "Would you play for me, Da?"

"Why, what a marvelous idea, Bobbi-lass!" His voice tender and loving as he released her hand and instead slipped his arm around her, giving her a gentle hug. "Shall I play for ye here, or do ye feel a mite adventurous? The day's glorious and Mathair has taken her lunch in the garden. Let's just get you settled with her and then I'll fetch Quicksilver."

Without waiting for an answer, he scooped Barbara up. He had her established on the padded lounger in the backyard before she knew what happened. Basking in the warmth of the sun, she could not protest. Barbara relaxed, embraced by a sense of pervading peace, as Conall bounded back into the house to fetch his fiddle, Quicksilver. Moira, her mother-in-law, followed him into the kitchen, emerging almost immediately with a second lunch plate, setting it beside Barbara with a contented smile. Conall quickly returned with the instrument. He began to play, kicking off an afternoon of laughing and singing in the sunshine.

For the first time in months, Barbara's fear lost some of its hold on her.

The release proved a balm to her soul as she felt energy flow into her on the melody, revitalizing every cell. Greedily she reached out to claim the unfamiliar strength...only to find her way blocked.

She would have nothing of that. Her spirit pushed and shoved until the barrier gave way, allowing her to claim that sense of power and potential she sensed around her, leaving her with the conviction that her future and that of her unborn child were no longer in doubt.

If her in-laws wondered at the serene smile gracing her lips, they did not question it aloud; they were too intent on watching as she lifted the sandwich from the table beside her, and with obvious enjoyment, devoured it.

Life was good, and Barbara marveled at her renewed sense of well-being as the music continued to weave its loving spell about her.

Conall was hard-pressed to understand what had begun that day. He well knew the level of his own mage talent, but what he could accomplish with his meager skill could hardly account for what he watched take place before him. He could feel a stirring in the currents surrounding the small gathering. Nothing malicious or harmful, but definitely bearing the aura of the fae. More: it was connected in some way to Quicksilver.

He nearly stopped playing. He had always known of the fiddle's nature, but what he sensed today was much more powerful than anything he'd noted in the past. It was as if some elemental force had slumbered unnoticed, deep in the grain of the instrument. That force woke now and with it a maelstrom of emotions: curiosity, sorrow, and an intense feeling of fierce, somehow maternal, love. The last spread with each note. He felt it wrap fleetingly about his own shoulders, emanating contentment and pride before moving on. The awareness barely brushed against Moira, showing only mild interest and acceptance, before enfolding Barbara in a shimmering, attentive envelope. The emotions spiked, darkening and deepening too quickly for him to gauge them. Barbara didn't seem to notice, but Conall took no chances. He didn't sense any malevolence, but that didn't mean there was no danger.

Conall O'Keefe mustered his ability and moved to warn off the magical presence he'd unleashed. Focusing his will through his music, he slipped his awareness past the fae force, interposing himself between it and Barbara. His fiddle transitioned into a battle anthem, leaving behind the softer melody of moments ago.

With a gentleness he would not have expected, the fae emanation reached out tendrils to extract him, gently removing the obstacle to its objective. Even now he could sense no malice, but it was fae and foreign, and he did not understand. Conall dug in his psychic heels and leaned back into his position, doing battle with his bow...only to have an equally determined awareness reach out to shove him away...from Barbara behind him. Confused and not a little disgruntled, Conall struggled to hold his ground, but even without Barbara's unexpected efforts on the behalf of the intruder, Conall could not withstand the fae. His mage skills dimmed, if only momentarily, almost taking his vision with them.

As he conceded, something astounding happened: the force he had foolhardily pitted himself against engulfed him and just as quickly released him. His bow faltered on the strings, and he trembled in the wake of the experience, but no longer did he doubt the benevolence of this entity; every whiff of energy he had expended in attempting to protect Barbara had been categorically replaced. So deep and all-encompassing had that brief connection been, that he would ever recognize, on an intimate level, the angelic being who had subdued him. He had no name for her, but he no longer questioned her intent: to love and protect his own family. The intensity of that love nearly floored him as he thought of the coming child.

His fae opponent seized upon his thoughts and once again reached for Barbara. Surprisingly, his daughter-in-law reached back, somehow bridging the gap between her ungifted self and the emanation.

Astounded, Conall watched with his second sight as the entity residing in Quicksilver galvanized and strengthened Barbara in every way possible. Gone were the doubts, gone were the fears, gone were the debilitating bouts of nausea and the air of frailty. The change was abrupt and astounding. He no longer had any doubts that in less than two months he would cradle his healthy grandchild.

A scream shattered the peaceful evening. Conall's heart took off like a trip hammer as he ran panicked out of the basement and up the stairs, the broken chair he'd been fixing completely forgotten. The kitchen stood empty, as did the living room, and he had cause to curse the fact that Moira had finally broken down and gone grocery shopping despite her fear of being away so close to Barbara's time. Even worse, Patrick had gone to work and wasn't due home for another two hours.

"Bobbi-lass…" Conall struggled to keep his voice calm and soothing as he took the stairs to the second floor two at a time. "Where are ye, love?" Another cry rang out, this time clearly coming from the upstairs bathroom. "Dear Lord…" he murmured, then louder: "I'm comin', Barbara!" He wanted to curse as he threw himself at the door, only to find it locked. "Unlock the door, sweetheart. Ye have to let me in."

"I c-can't get up!"

Damn! What had gone wrong? Conall wondered as he considered how to get the door open. Things had been going so well; Barbara was healthy and happy, with no further signs of the difficulties that had plagued her previous pregnancies. Now his past fears rallied from wherever they'd been hiding all these months. What was going on beyond this blasted door? If there was a key, no one knew where it was, and he couldn't break through it for fear of hurting Barbara, but maybe he could pop the lock; it was the safety kind with a small hole in the center to allow just that. He had to find something that would reach in far enough to trip the tumblers. A wire hanger should do it if he could find one. "Okay, love, I'll be right back an' see if I canna help ye up, ye just sit tight."

She didn't answer. Frantic, he ran into his bedroom and yanked open the closet door. All he found were those cheap, thick plastic hangers that used to be soda bottles in a past life. Blasted recycling!

What else? What else could he use? He looked around the room and spied Moira's bag of knitting. All the needles poking out were thick and nubby, but Conall seemed to remember a rather thin, fine one he'd had the misfortune to sit on some time ago. Pawing through her bag he found one. Without a second thought, he slid off Moira's stitches and ran back to the bathroom door, praying that the needle was thin enough.

In seconds he had the door unlocked. Carefully he pushed it open, fearful that Barbara might be in the way. She wasn't, but he didn't know whether or not to be grateful. The tub was behind the door. In the mirror's reflection, he could see the shower curtain half pulled down. He struggled not to moan. Whatever happened, he could not add to the fear she must be feeling, not if he wanted to help her.

"Da!" Barbara cried out as he moved further into the room. He could hear the terror in her voice and her breathing was erratic.

"Shhh...shhh...I'm here, Bobbi, I'm here." He closed the door behind him so he could reach her. The sight that met his eyes drained the color from his face; Barbara lay in the tub, her face pale and clammy and her distended belly rippling all too regularly. A trickle of blood crept down the side of her face and her pale blue eyes were dazed. Only the curtain protected her modesty. "Dear *Jea*-us! Barbara, what happened?"

"I don't know...I don't know!" Barbara sobbed weakly, and he could see the terror back in her eyes for the first time in months.

Dear God...let everything be okay. He doubted any of them would ever be the same if things went badly. Conall pushed the thought away as he reached over and turned off the shower, noting as he did so that his daughter-in-law had remembered to use the traction mat. Not a slip, then. Most likely dizziness or the onset of her obvious contractions had caused her fall. He reached out with the wet washcloth he found lying in the tub and gently wiped the blood from her face. "Are ye hurt anywhere else?"

Barbara shook her head but said nothing as another contraction took her. She hissed and clutched at her belly, her eyes pleading. To himself, Conall cursed. The contractions were coming too quickly...there was little chance of getting her to a hospital in time to deliver with all the conveniences and safeguards of modern medicine. In fact, if he didn't hurry his grandchild would be born in a worn-out cast-iron tub.

Conall tried to smile reassuringly as he reached to pull the curtain out of the way, talking all the while to keep her mind off her nudity, if nothing else. "Good...Very good. Okay, now...Let's get ye out o' there. Just hold me tight 'round the neck."

He braced himself as he slid his arms under her and lifted. She'd always been delicate; pregnancy had not done much to change that fact, but her bulk was awkward. He carried her carefully into her bedroom. Laying her down, he grabbed her nightgown and covered her. Only then did he take a quick moment to make her comfortable before circling the bed to the phone. His first call was to 911, his second to the docks where Patrick worked. Both the ambulance and his son were soon on the way. There was little else Conall could do but pray.

No, that wasn't true...he could take Barbara's mind off her worry. "Hey, love, help will be here soon..."

"Patrick!"

"Shhh...I've already called him," Conall murmured as he brushed back her tangled wet hair. "Just give me a moment, an' I'll be right back."

"No don't...*augh!*" Barbara spasmed again as she grabbed for his hand.

"Barbara, relax. It'll be all right, just hold on an' ride it through." He continued to soothe her as he carefully loosened her grip. "I'm going to get a few things we'll need until the ambulance gets here...I'll be but a minute. Okay?"

Fresh tears ran down her cheeks but she nodded. Conall hurried back into the bathroom for water and as many towels as he could manage. He wet a washcloth and draped that over his arm. Back in the bedroom he arranged the towels into a thick pad on the bed and shifted Barbara on top of them before using the washcloth to wipe the sweat from her skin. What she bore overwhelmed him. He couldn't imagine the strength it took to endure it.

"Ye're going to be fine, Bobbi-lass, everythin's goin' to be fine." The words sounded empty, powerless, even to his ears. Would fate be so cruel to let them come all this way, only to lose another one? "Shhh...ye just hang on, darlin'...Da's here."

Barbara managed a weak smile and took a sip from the cup he held to her lips. She looked like spun glass ready to shatter. "God! Why aren't they here?!" she cried through clenched teeth as her abdomen again contracted. "Talk to me...Do something, please?"

The moment the words left her mouth, Conall remembered that day four months ago when something fae had emerged from Quicksilver. It had touched Barbara; changed her. He was confident that was the reason this child was so close to being born, instead of going the way of the other babes. From that afternoon on, he had not let a day go past without fiddling some for Barbara. The violin, or whatever resided within it, called to him now and had been since he'd heard the first scream, though he hadn't realized it.

"Music, love," he was quick to suggest. "How about I play ye some music?" He barely waited for her nod before he dashed down the hall for Quicksilver. The case was propped in the window seat of the room he shared with Moira. He could feel the charge in the air as the fae spirit within waited for him impatiently. Without even stopping, Conall grabbed the case and hurried back to Barbara.

He had never unpacked Quicksilver with such haste before. Settling her beneath his chin he immediately tuned her and drew his bow across the strings. The change was astounding. Before the first notes faded, peace permeated the room, banishing the fear, stress, and doubt that had hung in the air like a *bean Sidhe's* wail. The atmosphere took on a fae glow; the notes fell off his strings in perfection though he played no composed work, just what flowed from his heart. He put all his love and hopes into the music, his eyes drifting closed as he focused on the magic he could feel unfolding. At once he prayed both to the God of his childhood and to the Mother Goddess of his otherworldly heritage...he prayed without end as the fae presence drifted toward Barbara, caressing her with pure energy, embracing her with intimate awareness.

With his mage sight, it was as if another woman had settled on the bed beside his son's wife and gathered her into insubstantial arms. There was a sensation that Conall had noticed each time he'd played for Barbara, but he was aware there was something wrong: it wasn't enough. Whatever watched over Barbara—angel or fae—it could not give enough without giving totally, and his daughter-in-law on some level resisted an absolute melding.

The fear came back, thick and heavy and oppressive.

"My baby! No! My baby!" Barbara screamed again and suddenly Conall knew the problem: as Barbara's doubts grew, her uncomprehending mind interpreted what was happening as a threat...as some force coming to steal or harm her baby. But that was wrong; he knew it deep inside. And yet Barbara fought the spirit with everything within her until Conall could see her fading even with his normal sight.

No! They had come so far; too far to lose the little one now!

Instinctively, desperately, Conall started to sing. He sang from the heart...not in English or Irish, but what he recognized as the ancient *Sidhe* tongue, which he had no cause to know. He sang of love and hope and unity against the darkness, and suddenly he did not sing alone. First one voice joined him and he knew it for Moira...then a second voice and it was Patrick... and a third, more ancient and awesome than anything he had ever encountered; the thought of putting a name to it was too terrifying to contemplate, though the knowledge hovered on the edge of his perception. That was the Fae One.

And magic blanketed the room. He scarcely knew how he managed to keep standing…let alone play. But continue he did, for the life of his grandchild…and surely all the rest of them… depended on it.

He could feel the moment the struggle ended. There were grunts and deep groans, during which Conall could not help but squeeze his eyes closed tighter. He was startled when Barbara's weak voice joined the chorus. Joy soared in a dazzling crescendo and like the sweet song of an angel, a babe's high, disgruntled wail rose from the bed.

Conall's eyes flew open, and Quicksilver nearly fell from his grasp. Two gasps from the doorway were proof he hadn't imagined the arrival of his family, but in this moment out of time he could spare no thought for them. Every ounce of his attention was riveted on the woman propped up in the bed before him. She wore Barbara O'Keefe's face, but the eyes that stared back at him were an unearthly green. The Fae One watched him with a calm serenity the likes of which Barbara had never shown. Conall's heart threatened to stop as he questioned if he might have been wrong. The woman in the bed smiled reassuringly as if his soul lay open to her—as well it may. Behind him, Patrick and Moira gasped again and he suspected they witnessed some glimmer of the ethereal beauty that smile unleashed.

Love infused the face that was both Barbara and not-Barbara, and Conall heard again the newborn wail that drew him back from the mists of magic. The child! Irrationally, doubt supplanted his conviction; all the tales he'd ever heard of changelings and the faeries stealing children flooded his thoughts. The child!

Immortal eyes now chided him, again from Barbara's face, and Conall knew shame. There was no deception in the melding that had taken place. As elf-kin, Conall knew better.

The Fae One's smile returned and love saturated the room; along with it came an influx of mage energy converging upon the bed. It gently encompassed mother and babe like a cloud until both glowed with it. Graceful arms cradled the perfect little creature and soft, borrowed lips leaned forward to plant a kiss on the pink little head with its faerie puff of dark curls. The child's whimpers and wails faded away and all were enchanted by its coos. Conall nearly fell to his knees in awe as the little one reached out a finger and with a pleased little gurgle drew the cloud of mage energy in like it was mother's milk. Satisfaction wreathed Barbara's face as the Fae One looked up and caught Conall's eye. He trembled beneath that regard, knowing, though no words passed between them, that there would be a day of reckoning somewhere down the line. They owed the spirit a boon for the miracle of this birth. As he nodded his head, green eyes lightened to blue and time came rushing back around them. In that instant, his right wrist burned as if wound by hot wire. Just briefly, then the sensation was gone. Conall swayed and trembled as Patrick forced his way past. Only the support of Moira coming up beside him kept Conall on his feet as they all welcomed wee Kara into the world.

The Promise of Death

"It is only the promise of death that makes life worth living."
– Robert E. Howard

AN RÓGAIRE RESISTED THE URGE TO RUB WHERE A CRESCENT-SHAPED ivory sliver yet marked his forehead, hidden by a dark shock of once-silken hair now gone rough. Just enough horn remained to serve as a stark reminder of all he had lost. Magic . . . kin . . . his true form . . . even his name. Everything but his life—which felt all but worthless without the rest—and his new-found purpose. A muscle in his cheek twitched as he raised his head and flared his nostrils to sample the air.

He caught a whiff, a mere memory of his quarry's scent, faint and growing fainter.

Tension radiated up his jaw as his teeth clenched. With each passing day, the threat grew that Den Jeger—brother to the man who had died severing An's horn—would figure out how to use it. Not an alicorn alive would be safe as long as Jeger held his trophy. Much like a dousing rod, the spire would lead the man to anyone nearby with even a trace of magic, alicorn or otherwise.

An could not let that happen. Just the thought drove him closer to the edge of madness as rage flared through him. He was more than a touch mad anyway, as most alicorns robbed of their horns—and thus their magic—tended to be, but for the most part, he was able to stay on the reasonable side of sane. In part because of the sliver of horn left to him, in part because he must. Forcing back the pain at the center of his forehead, An turned his focus outward and hunted the hunter, not for vengeance, but to neutralize the threat.

Jeger had to be stopped.

The energy of Dublin grated on An like a constant jolt applied directly to his nerve endings. He liked the city and had visited often over the years, but this constant exposure wore on him. What he wouldn't give to leave the perpetual barrage of traffic sounds, human voices, and electronic noise for the gentle music of the wild, to run on four legs and not two. Just for half an hour. Instead, Jeger led him a merry chase through the city. Over the last week, they'd stalked one another back and forth across every neighborhood in Dublin.

For now, An had lost track of the hunter. Snarling, he cut down an old, cobblestoned alley heading toward Trinity College, trying with the meager magic still at his call to locate Jeger's trail...or the spire's to be more precise.

An had been both blessed and cursed when he'd been cleaved. Once most rogues transformed to their human form for the final time—the only defense a hornless alicorn had in humanity's world—their ability for magic was spent. Not so for An Rógaire. The sliver he had left allowed him enough ability to glamour his features and cast other minor workings—such as sensing the inherent magic in others...and his horn, which Jeger had taken as a trophy. All An wanted was to retrieve the blasted thing and have done with this half-existence. No...that wasn't precisely true. What An *truly* wanted was to pound Jeger beneath his hooves until his fetlocks were crimson with the man's blood, to hear the man's screams fade away into the squelch of pulping flesh...

An's footsteps became more forceful in response to the violent thought and his lips twisted in a cruel smile until those walking toward him began to swing wide to go around.

As he realized it, he abruptly stopped, trembling as a cold, clammy sweat coated him. This was not him. This was not the behavior of an alicorn, whose nature was to heal, not harm. With each day that passed—and with him hardly realizing it—the madness took more control.

He needed to end this before it was too late. Before these impulses extended not just to Jeger, but to all mankind. Once the threat was gone, An could let go and find...release...from this shadow existence.

For that, he had to find Jeger.

Recklessly, he overreached himself, grasping for magic beyond his current capability. His stomach churned with the effort and a piercing pain lanced through his head. Slumping against a worn brick wall, he heaved a sharp sigh and pressed the heel of his hand against his forehead where the scar throbbed.

"Soundin' mighty vexed there, sunshine."

An jerked upright, his hand tightening into a raised fist. Aggression briefly surged through him, until he forced it back. As he regained control he recognized Charlie's voice and felt a phantom sensation down his back reminiscent of the tingling brush of another's magic. A sensation An had not felt since his cleaving. As his nerves settled he nearly snorted as the misnomer registered. But then, his friend here tended toward snark.

"Nearly missed you today, Charlie," An said in his gentlest tone as he forced his hand to relax. "Not finding trouble out there, are you?" As he spoke, he reached into the messenger bag slung across his shoulder and drew out what would have been his lunch. He managed an impression of a smile as he leaned out and handed it to the waif.

With a sullen look, Charlie jerked a hard head shake as she all but grabbed the sandwich. "Got more sense than that, An Rógaire."

He flinched. Though that alias predated his losing his spire, it was the only name he had claimed since. Being addressed by it left him feeling raw, as if he lost a little more of himself each time it was used.

Charlie didn't even notice, all her attention focused on the food. Deft hands extracted half the sandwich from the wrapper and squirreled the rest away, somehow managing to do so in a way that made it seem nothing was there at all. If not for her age and obvious state of existence, An would have suspected Charlie of being one of his kind, but no foal could have mastered the human transformation this young, and even if one had, they would have been sheltered and nurtured, not cast alone into the world to subsist among humankind at such a tender age.

Still...perhaps somewhere back in her human lineage she had alicorn kin. Despite living on the rough there was a sense of purity there, and signs of mage potential that might develop as she grew older. It was enough to make him wonder.

Of course, Charlie's entire nature was a puzzle to him. A long tenure on the streets had made her age and sex nearly indeterminate. Any tell-tale features were as hidden as the sandwich he'd given her. Most people assumed she was a young boy. An figured somewhere in her early teens and female, but that was just instinct. Her scent was muddied, not clearly one gender or the other. He'd known her for years through a mutual connection to the local Romani clan, but even he couldn't be completely certain, though he was better equipped than most at sensing biological cues.

Without intending to, he leaned a little closer and let his nostrils flare, still trying to make sense of Charlie's scent. She tensed and her jaw stilled. Though they'd known each other a while and counted each other friend, Charlie never lost the sense of self-preservation that kept her alive on the streets. She looked ready to drop the food in her hand and bolt.

An caught himself before she took off. He stepped back out of reach to lean against the opposite wall of the alleyway, sliding his hands into his pockets and crossing his ankles. It almost wasn't enough, but after a long, taut pause, Charlie lifted the sandwich and made half of it disappear in one bite, never once taking her eyes from him.

"What's the word?" he asked, knowing street kids—especially this one—were better informed than practically anyone else, just as a matter of survival.

That got him an eye-roll and half-shrug as Charlie carefully chewed, then swallowed before answering, showing she had more sense than most of those he sacrificed his meals too. An reached into his bag again and drew out a bottle of water, which Charlie was quick to take, but not snatch. She sipped enough to clear her throat before answering, then squirreled away the rest.

"The yobs are causin' trouble down by the docks, an' a new crop of Paki dossers are settin' shop 'round the market. I tell ya, they could teach them cinema actors a thing or two, they're that good at fakin'. Oh, an' someone's snatchin' school girls, but it's really strange. Always good girls...lily white, if ya get me. They turn up somewhere a few days later loopy on somethin' but otherwise just fine. Three's gone missin', an' two come back so far."

An bobbed his head and let her ramble between bites until her sandwich was gone. Normally, this was the point where they'd part ways. An hesitated. What she said about the schoolgirls concerned him, but that didn't sound like Jeger's thing. Yet anxiety twitched down An's back in an instinctive warning he couldn't shake.

It wasn't like anyone would confuse Charlie with a school girl. Hell, as far as he knew no one except him pegged her as female at all. If this was a random snatcher, An was pretty sure she was safe.

But what if this wasn't some random perv? What if gender wasn't the only common identifier between the victims? Jeger was out there somewhere roaming those streets Charlie called home. That made An nervous. He still couldn't say if his young friend had anything to worry about. Might be there was nothing more than the usual; unless his suspicions were correct and she was an aliman, a melding of their kind with threads of magic woven through her humanity. That could definitely put her more at risk from the hunter. The horn fragment Jeger possessed could lead him right to her, thinking she was an alicorn...and, worse yet, if she had any developing mage sense, she might not realize a stranger drew near if she felt An's essence through the horn.

Again violent urges surged through him. He closed his eyes as he felt them begin to roll and clenched his jaw as he swallowed down a bugling scream. Breathing slow and deep, he got himself under control before he spoke.

"There's a man out there you need to stay clear of..."

Charlie scoffed. "Just one, An?"

"I mean it, Charlie," he said, leaning forward to catch her gaze. "This guy's a hunter and might be you have enough in you of what he's hunting for." An quickly described Jeger, from his brush-cut blond hair to his flat brown gaze. He detailed the scar across the hunter's right wrist—for which An was unintentionally responsible—and even the horn shard—though An didn't call it that—which never left its custom-made sheath at Jeger's side. The way the man moved and how he operated. The words came out in a rush because An didn't know how long she'd let him talk before taking off. He could feel himself losing his calm with each word. Already her eyes were wary. "If you hear anything about him...or worse, cross paths with him, stay clear and get word to me through the Clan."

"Don't know what you're going on about." She started to back away and he knew she'd dash once she was clear of the alley.

"I just want you to be careful, Charlie. He's after me, but that doesn't mean you're safe if he notices you... If he notices what I have."

An spoke that last to the empty air.

Tension rippled through every muscle and drew his brow into a vicious scowl. An felt something looming on the air. As if there were somewhere he should be. Driven, he made his way across the Temple Bar. His hands fisted and his shoulders bunched as his gaze tracked all around him. Where was the bastard? It wasn't like Jeger to drop off the grid. To taunt and tease and try and lead An somewhere society wouldn't interfere, that was the hunter's usual course. But Jeger was nowhere to be found.

Jeger's absence left An agitated. But that wasn't all.

Over the past weeks, three more girls had been reported missing. They had all turned back up, in the same condition. Innocent girls, unharmed and intact, but with no memory of what had gone before. He had a bad feeling Jeger, misguided by legends of unicorns and virgins, was responsible for the abductions after all.

That wasn't why An was worked up, though. What had him worried was that there were only six girls reported missing. And seven had been found.

The seventh was a street kid no one knew or cared had gone missing.

An couldn't help but think of Charlie, whom he feared was number eight. The otherness about her reminded him of his own kind. The only other instance a human came close to such a resemblance—without possessing magic—was those who were pure.

Like all the other girls gone missing.

Alicorn had no care for human abstinence; what they sought was their own kind. Unfortunately, one form of purity often mimicked the other, giving rise to the legends.

The thought that the hunter might have targeted his friend kindled rage in An's belly. He felt the urge to roll his eyes and toss his head, rearing up in a display of equine fury, though his body could no longer manage the posture and his rough, shoulder-length locks hardly constituted a lashing mane. He fought the impulse down, but it kicked his ass. Even in the thick of Temple Bar foot traffic, the space surrounding An cleared. His nostrils flared with every heated breath and his lips kept twitching, baring clenched teeth. For a moment he caught his reflection and nearly screamed in challenge.

That snapped him out of it. He was no use to Charlie like this.

He wrestled the madness down and strove to ignore the depression that flowed into its place. He moved more methodically through the city with an eye out for the hunter but hoping to find his friend. He believed he caught fleeting glimpses of Jeger, occasionally sensing what might have been the trail of his horn, but An could not be certain. The presence of magic in the city and the crowds muddled his senses. There was enough whiff of Jeger's trail to lead An southward, but not give him a clearer sense of direction.

Giving up on the hunter, for now, An turned his focus back toward finding Charlie.

Gritting his teeth, he crossed the street toward St. Stephen's Green thinking to search the shadows beneath the trees, where the street kids like to hang after dark. Before he could dodge them, a cluster of women intersected his path. He grunted as he collided with a mass of soft curves and flowing skirts. Bell-like laughter rose in the night as two delicate hands gripped his arms to the musical clatter of a multitude of bangles. More laughter, just as loud and melodious rose around him until An cursed at the attention the bevy surrounding him drew.

"Ah, La-La! What a catch! Toss that one here if you even think of lobbin' him back."

"Now, now, La-La! Don't listen to her...family before all others, yeah, *cousin?*"

The catcalls and ribald comments continued as An sought to extract himself, but he stilled as soon as he recognized the Romani lilt to their voices and took heed of the name they called to.

"La-La?" he asked on a bare breath. He peered into the woman's face, finding familiar dark eyes asparkle among a riot of long, thick curls he knew would be a warm honey brown in the daylight. His hands came up to rest on her shoulders and hope seized his breath, scarcely believing to encounter this one here. She was not an alicorn, or even aliman, but she knew him and his kind. Her Clan...the Kalderaš Clan had oft sheltered members of his herd.

Perhaps...but no, he could not sense any kin among those with her. Still, the Clan might be able to help. They held magic of their own...for tracking, for Seeing. And they knew Charlie. Cared for her. If anyone could help him find the girl, it was the Rom.

The woman stilled, a frown on her face as she peered closer. He watched her gaze lose focus as her Sight kicked in and she saw beyond his glamour. Her eyes crinkled and her smile grew warmer.

"Lor...!" She started to squeal the name she knew him by, only An darted his hand out and pressed a finger over her lips, giving a sharp shake of his head. Jeger knew that name, but not the face An wore now to hide his own.

The sparkle in her gaze dimmed as she noticed the changes in him, along with his behavior. She scanned around them for trouble. Her forehead creased as none was evident, but any good Rom knew when best to be silent, and to fade from notice. She gestured to the women she was with. With a nod, they swarmed past the two of them, and moved off, their voices rising higher and more exuberant than before as they danced and laughed and drew everyone's eye off of the two they left behind.

An let La-La claim the hand he'd raised and draw him into the shelter of the boughs overhanging the wrought-iron fence surrounding the park. Together they turned and headed off in the opposite direction, both remaining silent and moving swiftly, once the attention of the masses was firmly anchored on the Romani women now playing "gypsy" to the hilt.

"Talk to me, my friend," La-La said once the crowds had been left behind, gently slipping her hand into the crook of his arm and reining him back to a more leisurely pace as they moved off down a quiet cobbled street. Her calm demeanor conflicted with the worry woven through her scent.

An stopped abruptly. He could not help it.

La-La turned back toward him. The worry blossomed in her gaze as she noted his faint trembling. He flinched when she peered closer at him, her brow furrowed. The muscles of An's face twitched as he tried to answer her, but he could not say the words. Could not tell her of his cleaving. She must have read something in his expression, though, because her hand rose slowly, as if not to startle, and gently brushed beneath the locks hanging heavy across his forehead.

He clenched his eyes shut at the sight of her silent tears as she mourned his loss.

"There is a hunter in the city...Den Jeger," An told her, his voice low and controlled, his tone flat. "He has gone to ground. I am afraid he has taken a friend of mine with him to force my hand."

As he filled the Romni woman in, fury kindled in her gaze. She reached out and took his hand, striding off with a determined gate.

"Where are we going?"

"Phoenix Park," she murmured. "The others need to know. An' perhaps we can help find...your friend."

As they made their way across the city the crowds lessened as the spaces grew more open. An turned his focus inward toward his meager trickle of magic and allowed La-La to guide him. Centering, he charged his senses and extended them outward, seeking Jeger's trail through the essence of the spire. His spirit surged. As they followed the Liffey toward Phoenix Park the trail strengthened.

La-La tried to draw him toward the Clan's camp, but An tugged his arm out of her grip. His nostrils flared as he caught the faintest trace of Charlie's scent wafting on the breeze. She was here, somewhere. Beyond Phoenix Park. Behind him, he heard the electronic tones of a cell phone dialing but ignored it, his stride lengthening as he left La-La behind.

An tracked Jeger to an abandoned warehouse in the Ballymount Industrial Estate, south of the city, past the park. A fire had left the building a burned-out husk not quite a year ago. The walls were solid, but the roof was gone in patches and the windows altogether. The gaps in the walls had been boarded over, but one had been pried away, left prominently propped against the smoke-scarred wall.

Through with games, An Rógaire stalked up the path between the buildings and straight to the way left open for him. He went alone, unwilling to risk the Rom in this private battle. Though he envied them the promise of death they and all mortals held, he would not be the cause of them embracing that state before they must. They'd trailed him anyway, he could tell by their scent on the air, but for now, they hid among the surrounding buildings. It galled him that he could not stop them, but he found it a comfort as well.

As he walked past a bunch of brambles closest to his target, La-La's voice whispered from the brush, "No fear, Lorcan. No matter what happens, the bastard won't walk away from this with your spire." Her vow touched him, as did her insistence on acknowledging his former self, but he could not let that distract him from his purpose.

"Go conquer your demon and when you're done you will return to the Clan so we may heal your hurts. You and your friend." He shook off her words and kept walking, but nonetheless, they warmed his heart. The Kalderaš Clan might not be his own, but their solidarity lent him strength...and hope, misplaced as it was. An Rógaire wasn't really concerned about walking away tonight, as long as Jeger didn't either, but to know Charlie had a place to be safe. He nearly reeled with the relief he felt at that.

La-La must have sensed his dark thoughts. She called after him in a low whisper, only loud enough to reach his sensitive ears. "I mean it, Lorcan. There is one known to the Clan who might help restore you...as she did me. Faerie-touched and magical as you are. She is called Anu..."

Anu? Surely he had not heard La-La correctly. One who bore the name of the Mother Goddess…? Powerful enough to restore him? His chest tightened as he longed to believe.

Forgetting the wisdom of silence, he pivoted to meet La-La's gaze. "What?!"

She nodded, but said nothing, as she drew back into her sheltering spot. He read the belief in her bright eyes before she fluttered her hands at him, shooing him toward the building. He continued forward, burying the seed of hope La-La had planted before it could distract him further.

As he drew closer to the warehouse the stench of old ash and moldering concrete assaulted his senses, overlaid by a heavy odor of industrial chemicals he could not identify either by origin or source. He marveled at the strength of it after all this time.

Huffing out his breath in an effort to clear the scents from his head, An climbed through the gap in the wall only to be assaulted by the odors ten-fold. How could they still be so strong? As he struggled against the overload, he was unsurprised to discover Den Jeger waiting for him. He locked gazes with the hunter and saw a mad glint in the man's eyes. Concerned, An resisted the urge to glance toward Charlie, slumped and bound to a chair in the middle of the vacant warehouse.

"Took you long enough to show up," Jeger said with a sneer. "I thought I'd have to try sheep next if neither girls *nor* boys served to lure you."

For a moment An was puzzled until he realized Jeger thought *Charlie* a boy. Puzzled enough that he almost missed the insult. An curled his lip in response, but he did not otherwise acknowledge Jeger's barb.

"You have something that is mine," An said, his voice freely channeling his wrath for the first time since the cleaving.

Jeger's hand moved over the ivory spire sheathed at his hip as if that was all that could possibly matter here. "Come closer, hellspawn. I'd be glad to give it back to you."

An could imagine all too well Jeger's meaning, envisioning his severed horn resheathed in his own chest, as it had once nestled among the ribs of this man's brother. That image haunted An. Alicorn were meant to heal, not harm, yet in his fear and his thrashing An had impaled the mortal intent on harvesting the very horn that ended him. And yet, Jeger's brother had not failed. Already partially hewn away, An's spire had snapped beneath the corpse's weight to become Jeger's trophy.

It would crush Jeger to know the death he dreamt of dealing this day was doomed to fail if the only weapon he'd armed himself with was the spire. The thought almost amused An, until the hunter interrupted.

"Time to pay for my brother's death, beast."

"There is no payment due, the thief owns the risk when he steals what is not his."

Jeger answered him with a rage-filled scream as he drew the spire and lunged forward. An nearly answered him, but Charlie's safety was dependent on An keeping his head. He flowed away from the path of attack with an echo of the grace he'd once had, barely resisting the instinctual urge to reach out and steady the man attacking him. How ironic, if Den Jeger were to impale himself. But no, the hunter pivoted and lashed out again, grazing An's arm. In an instant the wound healed, leaving a rent in An's sleeve, and nothing more, not even a crimson stain. The sensation of magic's caress nearly sent An to his knees as the blow itself had not.

"For you?!" Jeger spat, nearly foaming in his rage. "It still works for *you*?"

It was true. Once one, always one. Severed or not, the one person the spire would always heal was the one it had been cleaved from, of anything short of restoring the cleaved horn itself. Still, An was not about to try and explain the principle of sympathetic magic to his attacker. They were both haunted by the memory of that same horn jutting from the half-healed wound in the chest of Jeger's brother. The moment it broke free from An, it had lost its ability to heal as far as others were concerned.

He shrugged now, knowing it would infuriate the hunter, make him sloppy. "Maybe it was for old time's sake." In a calculated move, An held out his hand, palm up. "Come on, it is useless to you…"

"But not to *you*, which means I am all the more inclined to keep it." Hatred burned in Den Jeger's gaze. "Of course, there is one condition under which I would gladly return it to you." The hunter lunged and thrust once again. Even knowing it would fail to slay him, for an instant An felt the urge to fling his arms wide and bare his chest to Jeger's thrust. Shoving down *that* madness—more his personal demon than Jeger could ever be—An backed away, slowly circling. He focused every effort on drawing the hunter away from Charlie, who had come to and was working free of her bonds. As he carefully made his way through the wreckage left by the fire, fresh bursts of the earlier stench assaulted him. He glanced down and nearly stumbled as his gaze took in darkened concrete and glistening wood. Glancing back up, he saw two things that chilled him: Den Jeger, lost to madness, clutching a newly struck match; and Charlie, creeping up behind the hunter, a hand reached out to snatch An's spire.

At that moment, with La-La's words echoing in his memory, An Rógaire...no... *Lorcan* understood he had no more desire for death.

His or anyone else's...not even Den Jeger.

Leaping forward he grabbed for the match.

Startled, Jeger jerked back, his chemical-spattered clothes going up like a torch.

"No..." Lorcan barely murmured, anguish thickening his cry. "Charlie! RUN!"

She didn't hesitate. Even as Jeger shrieked in agony, with the kind of speed only a kid living on the streets possessed, Charlie snatched the spire from the hunter's grasp and shoved off in the other direction. But even she was not fast enough. An heard her hiss as she stopped short.

Already the fire had spread to every puddle and soaked surface until it crackled and snapped and roared at them from all sides. Charlie turned to An, eyes at once both panicked and trusting. He spied a patch of red, angry skin on her cheek where a bit of flame had licked too close. Crouching, coughing, he dove through the flames to reach her. Tucking her beneath the scant protection of his body, Lor searched for some way out.

He searched in vain.

And then he felt it. On his arm, where the spire Charlie still clutched brushed his skin, magic cascaded across his burns, healing them even as falling embers created more.

Once one, always one.

Dare he hope? Dare he not?

Unable to talk for the coughing, he reached out and took the spire from her hand and found the raw edge by touch. With a prayer to the Mother Goddess, he lifted the horn to his head, nestled it perfectly in place. Everywhere it touched, it tingled like crazy, but he knew it would not stay, and if it would not stay, this would not work. He could not take his true form and still hold the spire in place, assuming this was even possible at all.

Lorcan gathered his courage and vowed to live.

"Charlie...listen..." he lost his words in another coughing fit as the smoke grew thicker and the heat seized his throat. He shielded his face and tried once more. "Up on my back. Hold this in place and no matter what don't let go." He helped her clamber up as he choked out his commands, trusting she would either listen, or they would die.

She clung to him, trembling and crying silent tears, but with her hand steadfast as she held the spire to its base.

Lor closed his eyes against the sting of chemical-laden smoke and prayed again with every bit of faith he could muster.

The tingle became a burn of a different sort as magic flooded through him and Lorcan instantly transformed, tail flagged and mane thrashing, muzzle long and teeth bared as he challenged death with a defiant scream. Bunching his muscular hindquarters, he charged the flaming beast, his hooves ringing like steel on the concrete as they carried them through the open gap where he'd entered out into the cool night air to land among the Rom, who had swarmed the building and looked ready to charge the blaze.

For a brief instant, Lorcan was whole again.

And then he was not, as Charlie slid half-conscious from his singed back. Lorcan collapsed beside her, coughing great hacking coughs as he took on his human seeming once more. But, as he reached out a hand to cradle his dropped spire, Lor did not despair.

Because they were alive, and there was hope.

Forever and a Day

"A dream is a memory of what the future may hold
if you dare to reach for it."

DESPITE THE CENTURIES THAT HAD PASSED, TALA ATH COULD SEE THE image over and over like a flare burning against the lids of her closed eyes. The final ship at lift-off, rocket thrusters scorching the earth beneath with a fire that seemed to rival that of the distant sun. The vessel had been ancient but determined, resurrected for a final chance at glory by the last lingering remnants of the human race on Mother Earth. But for a few thousand scattered souls who had, with time, since passed on, mankind had departed for the heavens.

"Let the fools go," Declan's long-ago scorn echoed in Tala's mind in time with the vision. *"The Daoine Maithé will dance in celebration at their leave-taking."*

Tala's teeth clenched down upon the memory of her friend, cutting it off.

Talk about fools, she thought. *There are none so blind as those who will not see.* But oh, the horror in Declan's proud fae eyes when the truth came clear.

At first, the Earth had rallied, unfettered by the burden of humanity's disregard, freed from the bindings of pollution. For a time nature came again into its own as any soul would when a poison is drawn away. Around the world, flora and fauna both crept back from the edge of extinction, reclaiming the planet. Tala and her people rejoiced. Everywhere flourished such beauty as

had not been seen outside the fae lands since before the advent
of humanity. But eventually, in the early days of the Earth's
second century without Man, the initial effects were felt, gradual
but persistent. At first, things just leveled out, barely enough for
any to notice. But then it could not be denied that fewer young
were born among Earth's creatures with each decade that passed
and less of fruit and flower came from nature's bounty until even
the fae in their sheltered Lands sensed the lessening of all things.

In the absence of mankind's fleeting vibrancy...their passion...the spark that set them apart from all other of Earth's
children, nature seemed divest of its sense of purpose. Without
the humans' life force and the mage energy sloughed off from
them like skin to dust—vital to the ecological balance—those left
behind faded. The animals, the plants, and even the fae, though
many decades passed before any acknowledged the cause.
Declan had been among the first. Though not truly dead, he and
others like him drifted into a stupor state from which none woke.

It could no longer be denied: Without humanity, the Earth
and all it held were doomed.

With a frustrated huff, Tala turned away from the remnants
of the ancient launch pad. Careful steps led her through the
crumbling infrastructure of what she was told used to be the
Kennedy Space Center. Over the remains of ivy-draped concrete
blocks and steel supports rusted through until they appeared
like lace, across the memory of long-gone tarmac and past where
a stray shard of glass somehow clung to its twisted aluminum
frame, Tala's darting gaze sought out the odd jay nesting in
crumbling rafters and faded blossoms long-reverted to their wild
state rooted in the rich loam of rotted timbers. Her fae heart
cringed at the faint yellow cast to the grasses over which she now
trod. It had taken centuries, but like a field sown season after
season with the same crop, something vital was missing from the
Earth and everything that grew upon it.

The planet had lost a piece of its soul and heaven help them
all if it could not be gotten back.

Tala continued on her way before the ache grew too much to
bear. As she did so, a trill gave her faint warning to brace before
a small, compact form collided with her calves and took her to
the ground.

"Beag Scath!" she scolded, but with little heat. She found it difficult not to smile as the sprite wove his head fetchingly, sending his tousle of multi-hued locks bobbing. He grinned and scampered up her limbs to perch by her shoulder.

"Now, what are ye on about?" she asked, meeting the little one's orange gaze. He fussed and didn't speak, but then he seldom did. He was an odd one, bold and brash and long-beloved, having attached himself to Tala's Clan centuries before. Originally companion to the *Sidhe* who'd called herself Maggie McCormick, he'd glommed on to Tala's grandmother when she first became Maggie's charge and protégé. That was during the ancient days in New York when Maggie served as both pawnbroker and one of the guardians of that city. Or so Tala had been told in many a bedtime tale.

As if in reaction to her thoughts, Beag Scath reached out with a minute hand to clutch her ear while he leaned forward and brushed a kiss across her forehead.

Suspecting the wee one had not just capriciously bowled her over, Tala closed her eyes and reached out with her thoughts. *Mamó, did ye tell the little monster to dump me on my arse, or was that his idea?*

A dry chuckle and a thread of music teased her inner ear before her grandmother responded from somewhere behind her. "Sorry, *lhiannon*, he got away from me."

Tala tilted her head back to spy her grandmother, Kara-Anu, looking as youthful as Tala herself, with bright amber eyes and a mane of deep red hair curling around and past her shoulders. The case holding her enchanted violin, Quicksilver, hung by its strap across her back, half hidden by those wild tresses. The grin on her grandmother's face woke an answering one on Tala's. "Hi, Mamó."

"Hi yourself. Now up with you, my child, we haven't time for lying about."

Her brow wrinkled in confusion, Tala clambered to her feet. She had to scramble to keep up with her grandmother, who immediately set out across the clearing back toward the remnants of the launch pad.

"The memory of this place is strong even now," Mamó said as Tala came up beside her. "It might just do."

"Do for what?"

"You've cousins among the Kalderaš Clan...it's time you met them."

Kalderaš! Romani travelers. The first to venture forth from the Earth; driven to the stars by prejudice and their race's curse to wander. Tala had grown up on tales of the courtship between the steadfast Jacko and his Sidhe bride, Agnieszka, of the torment of Tony DeLocosta (possessed by an evil demigod and nearly lost in that one's banishing), and endless stories both bright and dark of their children and their children's children. She had never met even one of them, born only after the Rom had journeyed to the stars. Her heart thrilled at the thought of meeting cousins born from those cherished figures.

"How?" she asked, turning eager eyes upon her grandmother.

"Come," Mamó beckoned. "It's time to build new dreams of the old." And she showed Tala her vision as only the *Sidhe* could. Of the wandering Romani race finally gaining a home, of the Earth revitalized with the return of her wayward children. Of the world and all it held growing hale and whole and healthy once more. Tala's breath left her in a rush through open lips and her eyes went wide in awe. But without question, she followed. This would not be the first time Mamó had saved the world, though few but the fae knew the truth of that other tale. Tala had grown up expecting wonders of Kara-Anu, the mortal girl who had become both fae and goddess.

In the center of the crumbling launch pad, crowded by the memories of long-ago dreams, Tala watched as Mamó cradled Quicksilver beneath her chin and brandished her bow. And then bow arm stroked and fingers danced until Kara-Anu's whole body moved with the power of the song. Tala's spirit calmed until she found herself first humming, then singing, drawn into the spellcasting. Melody and harmony wove about them in a dance of color and light and music such as the world had long done without. The air crackled with the gathering magic. Tendrils and sparks lit up the space surrounding them, music wrapped them in its grip with silky smooth notes that ran like fingers over their hair, raising the strands like burning clouds about their heads. Raw energy ready to do their bidding.

Together they wove a vessel of starlight and moonbeams, of sunshine and life force, powered it with resolve and bound it all tight with their will until before them rested a glittering orb stretched oblong like a grain of fat rice. A touch to the shimmering skin sent rainbow ripples across its surface. Those ripples murmured an echo of the melody woven into the craft's making.

Tala released a quavering breath. What a glorious thing.

"Are you ready, Tala?" her grandmother asked. There was a faintness to her voice that made Tala frown, but she nodded. Mamó ran her fingers along the edge of the orb, folding away a section of the skin. She held out her hand. For a brief moment, Tala could not bring herself to take it but this was her grandmother, the undying Kara-Anu, soul sister to the Mother Goddess Danu herself.

Tala allowed her grandmother to aid her into the vessel of light and life. It cradled her as she had not been since she was a child small enough to fit in her Mamó's arms. Tension melted away in the warmth of that embrace. She looked around for Beag Scath, wanting to say farewell, but the sprite was oddly absent, though Tala swore she could faintly hear his cooing. With a frown, she turned her attention back to her grandmother. From where she stood outside, Mamó caressed the orb. "This will get you where you need to be." She paused to draw a cord from around her neck. From it dangled a familiar copper pendant etched with faint runes. "And this will guide you."

The medallion...it was an ancient charm that in ages past had linked a younger Kara to the Romani before they were kin. It had been given to Mamó by one called Granddame Rose, grandmother to the demigod-possessed Tony. As it settled over her head, Tala sensed the kernel of power still nestled in those protective runes just as binding as the day they'd first been etched. If tears glistened in her eyes at that gift, her jaw dropped at what came next.

"And she will keep you safe," Kara-Anu decreed with a hard edge of command backing the words as she slipped Quicksilver and her bow into its case, and the case into the space by Tala's feet.

Tala did not argue, but she did ask, "The Kalderaš, what am I to tell them?"

Kara-Anu remained silent a moment, her eyes glimmering as she leaned forward, pressing a kiss to Tala's forehead. "Tell them...It's time to come home."

Travellin' Show

GYPSIES, TRAMPS, AND THIEVES...IT WAS THE TITLE OF AN ANCIENT song from the twentieth century that echoed with my voice, my life—for all that the singer was a woman, and planet-bound. She and I shared the same nose, and perhaps a dark, unfathomable gaze, but not much else, other than the soul of that song. I don't even know her name, though we had fragments of old dig-vids of her singing the words in deep, whiskey-rich tones.

I hated her for seeing so clearly. For making me see so clearly.

For many Ages of Man, the human race had longed for the stars. I had them and didn't much care for it. Me, I wanted dirt beneath my feet miles deep, moving in a slow, massive spin I couldn't hope to feel were I as still as dead. I wanted to look up and see the stars twinkle and find nothing but satisfaction in the fact that I could see them through the filter of a planet's sky. I wanted roots, just once in my life, if only for a moment.

I believed someday I would. Someday...if I had to live up to every rotten thing they said about us. The kindest folk said we were all glitz, glam, and sham; everyone else...well, you get the idea.

You see, the frontier of space was much more dangerous than any similar state of existence planetside. People were desperate, harsh, and took what they could get as a way of easing the darkness all around them. They got to believing everyone else would gladly do them worse, so do it first.

That's why there are rules that every Caravan holds to and ruthlessly enforces. Cheat us, and we're gone; harm us, and we're gone for good; kill one of our own, and don't ever sleep again.

The dark is deep and cold. We—the Rom—are a touch of golden warmth in the black, a laugh when the universe is crying, passion where most bodies are worn down to indifference. We are welcome everywhere...once night falls and the stage lights are lit, the carnie booths are pitched, and everyone young and decent is tucked away in bunks. We bring the things that can't be had, the little pleasures, moments of forgetfulness, news from home ironically delivered by those who have never had one, unless you count the caravan ships.

No matter how they looked down on us, there wasn't a man jack in space who would risk being stricken from our travel circuit by mistreating us.

Or so we believed.

"Paolo, come on...it's time to dock." Terlinda startled me as her voice crackled from the wall comm. My sister sounded annoyed.

I said nothing and finished shaving, rebelliously scraping an antique straight razor across my scalp with slow care, revealing smooth, bare skin that was every inch a lie. On the Kalderaš Caravan, there wasn't a patch of skin on any of us above the age of three that wasn't tattooed with vibrant, nanite-embedded ink. Some claimed it was because in space we couldn't paint our caravans as our ancestors did, so we patterned our skin instead.

Maybe that was true, but more importantly, the tattoos were both warning and defense, though none but our own were aware of the latter. As far as the universe was concerned it was just one more difference between us and them. An easy way to tell who not to trust...or piss off, but other than that, just elaborate skin art.

Little did they know.

The markings of the Rom did more than earn us those labels of glitz, glam, and sham...at a silent mental command the nanites in the ink projected sensory holograms, creating the illusion of hair, clothes, and even ready-changing features by means of hard-light holo-projections intricate enough to fool even complex electronic recording devices. Mostly we used it to enhance our performances, but it came in equally handy when we had a need to vanish without a trace or appear as something other than what we are.

The universe knew us by our ink. This is why—when not among the *gadje*...outsiders—my silent protest was to appear unmarked by any color that wasn't flesh and to retain the growth of hair most of my people had chemically switched off as a practicality of traveling in space. Yes, it meant I had to shave before docking with other vessels or outposts for a show, but I still held the hope that my life would be different someday, and even just that fringe of hair that was not illusion made me feel it might be attainable. Little did *I* know.

"Paolo! Now!" This time Terlinda snapped at me from the cabin hatch, sending my hand and the razor it held sluicing sideways in a shallow cut across my scalp.

"Sh!" I hissed with the pain, however brief; I felt a sharp tingle cross my damaged skin as diligent nanites rushed to repair their roof. Glaring back at her I took the time to clean the blade and carefully put it away before rinsing the blood and shaving foam from my head. In moments, the only clue I'd bled myself was the fading metallic tang on the air.

"What is the point of all of this?" she asked, her hand gesturing at my illusion of normalcy, annoyance and exasperation coloring her words. "It isn't like you will ever fit among them, no matter what you look like. All you do is waste our time. And cost us double docking fees for holding up station traffic."

I didn't bother to argue anymore. It was an old battle of strike and counterstrike etched into the temporal memory of the ship a thousand-fold. In silence I moved past her, lowering my head to kiss her brow—which annoyed her further, as I'd had a growth spurt that left me six inches to the advantage of her own five-feet. While she sputtered I strode down the corridor toward the docking portal and my assigned task. We were not at risk of fines, despite Terlinda's claims; not this time and never again since the first time, before I'd learned to feel the changes in the drive that indicated power-down in preparation for docking. Since becoming attuned to those subtle variations in the engines' sounds I have never, ever been late to my post.

Terlinda growled behind me, her breath huffing ever so slightly as she hurried to catch up. "Are you so ashamed of what we are that you want to be like them? Are you so eager to be *gadje*?" She spat the word, a bitter insult when applied to one of our own.

What she said stopped me, but it was what I heard beneath the words that had me turn back to her. Her surface scorn mingled with a deeper hurt that she tried to hide, bringing glimpses to the surface. I met her eyes, so like my own, deep and dark, if rather more deceptively doe-like. I closed my own against the pain she let me see there. It nearly gutted me to be the cause of it. She was like my own mother, for ours had long ago joined the stars as we never could this side of life. How to explain to her and not hurt her more?

"*Camlo*,"—*lovely one*—"there is nothing about shame in this...of any of you or myself." I struggled for the words to explain what I had yet to make clear to anyone in my clan. "Have you never dreamed to stand upon a planet? To feel its unmoving mass beneath your feet? To see the grass and birds and a proper sunrise? To breathe the crisp, clean flavor of natural air and not feel the constant threat of vacuum weighing down on you?"

For just a moment in my life, I wanted to know what it felt like not to wander. Had my sister never felt the same?

Before she could answer me, the rumble of the engines shifted to a subtle drone warning me I'd no more time. I left Terlinda with confusion in her gaze as I spun around and hurried to my post before I proved her right about the fines.

The Midway Outpost was exactly that: midway between Earth and the furthest colony. It orbits a planet called Xerxes where there are a few scientific installations and one military complex, but not much else, according to the spatial-net. I have never been there before—the planet or the outpost. It takes a long time to tramp around the universe. The last time the Kalderaš Caravan had docked here was sixteen years ago; I had not even been born.

With a swiftness gained by much repetition, we unloaded our wares and trappings from the ship and shuttled everything we would need to set up our traveling show to an emptied assembly bay at the center of the outpost.

Whether founded or unfounded, the reputation of our kind preceded us. We were watched over closely as we went about our business. Some of us too closely. Each time Terlinda left the Caravan the eyes of the male outpost personnel followed her. I did not like the looks on their faces. Though I was only fifteen and my sister nearing twenty, I knew as her brother it was my place to protect her. What was more, I loved her as I loved none other, and God help anyone who offered her insult or harm.

When she next came down the ramp I walked beside her wearing the appearance of a man taller and more muscled than I could ever hope to be. The tattoos on the seeming—different from those on my actual body—were bold and aggressive, all stark black lines and bright blues and reds, like the warnings given off by the skin of a poisonous toad. I didn't need any help from the nanites to darken my expression as I made sure to catch the eye of each of those men staring. Some of them looked amused and went back to what they were doing, others sneered and kept on looking, some rare few were clearly embarrassed and nodded respectfully in our direction before turning away; none of them challenged my silent warning.

And still, for the balance of the offload I kept that image of power and strength. The effort wore on me as I had to remember my perceived physical boundaries, as opposed to the actual ones.

"You are an ass," Terlinda murmured under her breath at me.

"Love you too," I grumbled back while maintaining my looming presence and ducking under a hatchway that I would have otherwise walked beneath with no problem. The others of the clan politely took no notice of my ruse, though for one who knew how to tell they were clearly amused.

Finally, with the pack-out complete, we set about transforming the lackluster bay into a cross between a gypsy carnival and a homeworld bazaar. Lights and bobbles and fabrics in bright, vibrant colors were swiftly deployed and arranged. Right at the entry hatch the other boys and I set up the three-sided square of stalls. The moment we finished one the older women filled it up with luxury goods while we moved onto the next. The stalls were simple frames of aluminum 'bamboo' draped with colorful silk.

In addition to ambiance, they served to block the view and path of those who had not paid to enter the carnival. Beyond this screen, Father and my uncles were raising two larger, more private tents, off to either side of the bay—one for business such as the sending and receiving of personal messages, discreetly purchasing certain goods, or treating ills the crew could not or would not bring to the Medbay; the other was for entertainments for which the crew must pay an extra fee to view, such as the fancy dancing and the curiosity acts. Beyond all of that, the rest of the space was for feasting and public dancing. The younger women were in charge there and had already created of the bare, serviceable bay an exotic gathering area that bore little resemblance to its earlier state.

Wiping the sweat from my holographic chin—in truth, my damp brow—I watched as my sister and cousins set up the fireboxes, our version of the traditional firepits that would have been found at a true carnival. Already the scent of spices and meat were on the air and they hadn't even started cooking. My mouth watered. At a table beside her, other women of the clan set out specialty foods that would soon go on to the encased grill as regulations forbid open flames in the oxygen-rich canned atmosphere of the outpost.

Terlinda laughed as she stoked the coals and started loading prepared kabobs in the transition area to be moved on to the grill. She made a face at me when she caught me staring. I didn't mind because her eyes were filled with love; it was good to see her without the scowl I usually managed to put on her face. Turning away I bent to clean up the last of the tools we had used to set up the bazaar. As I did, I noticed one of the watchers from earlier nearby. His gaze hooded...one corner of his mouth barely upturned. I did not care for what I saw. The man watched the women preparing the food.

"Can I help you?" I asked, stepping between him and them.

He smirked. "Naw, just working up an appetite."

My jaw tightened at the many ways that could be taken. "If you don't mind, we aren't quite ready for business yet. Thank you."

"So, tell me," the man said, his expression growing sly and a touch hungrier. "Which tent do we go to for a little time with one of the girls?"

It took an effort to keep my tone neutral. I may not have succeeded. "None of them. Romani women don't sell their virtue."

The crewman looked confused, and then angry. I was fortunate that I still wore my more intimidating, if illusionary, seeming from earlier or perhaps things would have gone differently. As it was, he lifted his chin and just barely his lip in the ghost of a sneer, his arms crossing over his chest. In response, I sent a subtle command to the nanites beneath my skin to flex my holographic muscles. I held the man's gaze. I saw evil in the soul staring back at me.

Things could have gotten ugly if the station's head of security had not come through the hatch as we stared one another down. The watcher's gaze flickered to the newcomer; mine stayed steady on the man.

"Everything okay, Crewman Tran?"

"Yes, sir," Tran answered as his arms dropped to his side and he turned to salute his superior. It was then that I noticed the security patch on his uniform and cursed beneath my breath. "Just about to inspect this gypsy's load, make sure nothing that belongs to the station *accidentally* got mixed up with it."

I must have growled at the offense because both the crewman and his boss looked at me intently.

"Paolo," Father's voice cracked sharply from behind me. "Let security look, then get those tools back to the Caravan and put away."

With a subtle understanding, the head of security gave a little wave of his hand, a polite smile on his face. "No, that won't be necessary. I'm sure you all have plenty to do to ready things for tonight. We won't hold you."

Startled, I looked up and met his eye. His smile deepened into one with more warmth. I suddenly got the impression I didn't fool him. He nodded toward the hatch and stepped to the side. As I walked away, slightly trembling in reaction, I spared a glance for my sister; she looked safe and happy, surrounded by our family as they finished the final preparations for the carnival. With that sight firm in my mind, I was content to turn and go.

As I moved down the corridor I heard the officer speaking behind me: "Tran, your new orders have come in. You're being rotated planetside; report to the XO for your papers and a shuttle requisition."

I resisted the urge to turn and smirk back at that asshole, who would now miss out on all the carnival did have to offer.

It was petty, but my only satisfaction.

By the time I stowed the tools and endured the latest lecture from my father, who had followed me back to the Caravan, it was time to change. The carnival had been running several hours and shortly the special performances would begin. I once more appeared as myself, brightly colored and intricately marked, swirls and ancient markings clear upon my skin, with a starburst at the center of my forehead that subtly sparkled as the nanites beneath the skin released tiny charges of light like controlled static, only without the shocking sensation. My garb, while suitably flamboyant in cut, was subtle in color. I wore a long open vest of raw amber silk belted over a crisp, white shirt with billowing sleeves and a front that opened in a deep vee to my navel. My pants were supple black leather that just barely gleamed in the subdued light of the carnival. They were close-fitting but soft as kid and no impediment to movement; no small consideration, as I was a tumbler tonight. Finished with my preparations, I went to join the rest of the special performers, who were gathering at the exit ramp.

It disturbed me not to see my sister. She loved the life we led, the performing, the glamour, the thrill. In all my given memory I couldn't recall a time when she hadn't been the first to the ramp, in her jewel-tone scarves and bangles, flowing skirts and soft, curl-toed slippers. My eyes scanned the group again. All there, but for Terlinda.

"Father..." I called. There must have been some warning in my voice.

He turned from where he talked with Uncle Tomias, the two of them reviewing the entertainment planned for the night, as they always did. Father's brow gathered in concern, the pattern there wrinkled with the expression. "Paolo?"

"I don't see Terlinda."

I could not read his expression, which disturbed me, but his tone remained calm as he said, "Go check her cabin, please." I hurried to do as he bid.

She was not there. But her costume was, waiting on a peg beside her door, ready for the night's performance. I snatched one bangled scarf and hurried back to where my family waited. I did not even have to speak.

As if I even could.

My father ordered me to stay behind. He knew. He knew better than I did what would happen if he let me free. If we discovered the worst.

I tried to obey. I told myself that I should be there when she returned, as surely she would. My Terlinda should not come back to an empty ship with whatever grief she may have suffered.

No. I should not think such thoughts. And yet my heart knew no innocent thing had kept Terlinda from all she loved in life. Guilt burned like a brand inside me. I paced and tore at my clothes, battered my mind for any clue hiding there. My thoughts kept coming back to Tran and the look in his eye. The sickness in his soul.

There was no staying put.

Throwing off my costume I pulled on an outfit of all black cotton, close and tight as a second skin, nothing to impede me, whatever I must do. From a locker beneath my bunk, I drew a matching set of antique throwing knives I'd inherited from my grandfather, and he from his. They were the only things I had that resembled weapons. I'd been well-taught in their use.

I normally only used them when I performed one of the curiosity acts.

Without a second thought, I belted them around my waist. An order to the nanites both hid them from view and cloaked my features in a nondescript face made up of pieces melded from the crew, creating an appearance vaguely familiar but known to none. Armed and armored against resistance I circumvented the lock on the hatch and went out into the station, seeking out the only one who might help me.

Even armed with the directions to his personal cabin, it took some time to find the head of security. More than it had taken to find his name—Stan Wilkes—which I carefully pilfered along with the rest of my information from the station system using hacking skills learned at my granddad's side.

Wilkes did not seem surprised to see me.

"I expected you sooner, Paolo," he said, as I slid through the hatch to his cabin.

I went still, the holo image fluxing around me in my confusion. Then the man blinked and I could clearly see the flutter of lenses flick across his eye. I dropped the seeming.

"I wouldn't be a very good head of security if I didn't have the latest tech, would I?"

He started to rise. I locked my jaw and braced myself for an attack, but he sat back down, placing his hands in full view palm down upon his desk. "It's okay. I'm not against you. Your father has been to see me," he explained. "My men are searching now, your people with them; I'm only here to review the security feed, or I would be searching right along with..."

I cut him off. "It was Tran."

Wilkes sighed and lowered his head in acknowledgment. When he looked up I wanted to snarl at what I saw. "It was him!" I stalked forward, my fists clenched and my expression as twisted as my gut. My sister was in the hands of a beast, I had no doubt, and as clear as I knew that, I knew just from looking at him that the man before me was going to say there was nothing he could do.

I blinked and stopped dead. Without seeming to move at all, Wilkes had drawn a riot gun on me. I cursed and stood there trembling, waiting for the door behind me to open and security forces to hurry in. Instead, Wilkes placed the non-lethal weapon on the desk and slowly rose to his feet.

"I suspect you are right, but I can't prove it, and Tran left the outpost less than twenty standard minutes after I sent you back to your ship. The feed *seems* to support that he left alone."

My knees buckled at his words. I would have fallen without the edge of the desk.

That had been over four hours ago. That was when I understood Wilkes's expression: his men weren't on a search and rescue. They were on a search and *recover.*

Something inside me wanted to howl. To scream and cry and curl into a ball. That something was frozen in ice, locked deep down at the angry core of me. I locked gazes with Wilkes and waited for him to say what I knew was to come.

His voice sounded just above a whisper. "I can't go after him based on the feed, even though I suspect it's been altered...any more than I could go after you for stealing a shuttle *if the feed said it wasn't you.*"

I straightened, then nodded, before turning and walking out the door.

By the time I hit the corridor, I wore another face.

Hijacking a shuttle was easier than it should have been. But I guess I shouldn't have been surprised; after all, the head of security was unofficially supportive of my efforts. Still, it felt like a cheat. Not that I dwelled on that then, not with my sister's well-being dependent on my success. Or so I told myself.

There wasn't anyone among the Rom above the age of eight that didn't know how to pilot a shuttle. Personally, I could fly anything, up to and including the Caravan itself. A shuttle was nothing. Now figuring out Tran's flight path...that took a little more finesse. Not the one he'd logged with flight control, but the one the tracer in his craft automatically recorded. Most people didn't even know those existed.

I'm not most people.

Even so, an ordinary hack wouldn't have gotten me the data. That was why I'd lifted Wilkes's security code earlier when I figured out where to find him. I suspect even then I'd had his unofficial support.

I'd just left the stratosphere when the tracker on my shuttle pinged the one Tran had taken to the surface. It appeared by the mapping display that he had set down in a secluded clearing about ten miles from the complex he had been assigned to. I tried not to think of why.

It never occurred to me I was, in part, about to achieve my dream. I was too focused to really notice. Or wonder. Too tormented to care.

The more I descended the harder it was to breathe. The more my heart pounded. The harder it was to think. I dropped my engines as low as I could without stalling and glided the craft in, landing about a quarter mile from Tran's location, out of sight of the shuttle.

The hatch on my vessel cycled open and I barely felt I had the strength to climb to my feet. The pull of full gravity was like granite ballast filling me up. The air burned my lungs as I screamed in rage. I had not considered the effects of planetfall on a body that had never before left space.

I forced myself to my feet and somehow made it to the open hatch. If my body were not well-honed by the rigors of performance I could not have managed even that.

I did not so much climb to the surface as tumble down the stairs. The natural light nearly blinded me. When I manage to gain my feet, slow step by slow step, I dragged myself in the direction of the other shuttle. The hatch was open when I got there. I just stood and stared, scarcely believing how both simple and hard this journey had been. In truth, I dreaded what I would find. Dreaded more what I might not. What if she wasn't here? What if I had made the wrong choice and Terlinda suffered for it?

I gritted my teeth and climbed the steps to the shuttle hatch. I was no more than halfway when a sound came to my ears. Snoring. Faint snoring, broken up by a snuffle and occasionally a murmur.

Yes, it took me that long to climb.

When finally I reached the top I slumped against the hatch, not caring if my quarry should see me. It took forever for my eyes to adjust again to darkness.

Inside, deep at the angry core of me, I died.

On the floor of the shuttle lay Tran fast asleep and naked.

Beside him...my Terlinda, her eyes vacant and filmed, the damage to her bare body half-knitted by the nanites before they too began to die. The colors of the ink beneath her skin were fading without the bots inner brilliance. Tears streamed down my face, but I did not feel them. My chest heaved and my eyes glazed; I did not even realize as my right hand fell to the hilt of one of my throwing knives.

Tran twitched and snorted, and some benumbed portion of my brain railed at the wrongness of that. Muscles and reflexes trained by countless performances and an even greater number of practices fought against the weight of gravity to do as they had been taught.

The Caravans hold to a code: Cheat us, and we're gone; harm us, and we're gone for good; kill one of our own, and don't ever sleep again.

We would never return to Midway Outpost.

I would never again set foot on dirt.

We left in the night. It was simple, even on a fortified outpost, as long as you had the skill to bypass the systems keeping you in dock. I did, but I wasn't in any shape to. Hell, I didn't even know how I'd gotten us back. That didn't quite matter, though, as we seemed to have retained certain unofficial support.

Someone else stepped up and unlocked the gate.

In the finest tradition of gypsies throughout history, we faded away among the stars like a memory to protect one of our own.

That would be me. Paolo.

I killed a man, a *gadje*, a vicious dog who behaved worse by far than anything people said of us. I don't even know his first name. Frankly, I don't care. What I know is that he brutalized my sister and she died at his hand.

Tran should have remembered not to sleep.

The Devil's Own Luck

I LEFT THE KNIVES BEHIND. EVERYTHING I HAD LEFT IN LIFE HAS BEEN ripped away because I left the knives behind. Pain born of more than exile tore at Paolo's chest worse than the frantic clawing of lungs in vacuum. He was sixteen and all alone in the universe. Too drained to resist such despair, he huddled in the little pocket of space he'd carved out in the center of the stacked cargo. Storage containers shielded him top, bottom, and sides as he gave in to the silent tears burning their way past his frozen soul. He leaned against the molded plastic crates, not even caring if they shifted with his weight, halfheartedly wishing they would tumble, crushing his body as life had done his spirit. His sister would have scolded him.

How he wished by everything he'd once held sacred that she still could.

Terlinda's compressed ashes rested heavy against his heart. He tempted fate by keeping them close, but could not bring himself to let her go. The remnants of her physical self would surely draw her *mulò*—her ghost—to him. Would that be a blessing or a curse? He could not say. All he knew was the black velvet pouch containing the cube of her remains wrapped in her favorite scarf served as the sole touchstone left to Paolo's life before he'd killed a man, sliced him from neck to nut sac with antique knives passed down in his family for generations. Knives as distinctly Romani as the nanite-infused tattoos scrolling every inch of Paolo's skin. Knives he had left buried deep in the corpse.

Might as well have signed his name.

None among the Kalderaš Clan held blame against him, but the Rom had a saying: *family before all others.* When a friendly dockmaster warned them that the military base on Xerxes had deployed forces in pursuit of the Caravan, Paolo slipped away at the next refueling station, determined to protect his remaining loved ones. He'd made it as far as the outpost orbiting Io before the grunts caught up with him. After that, it had been one near miss after another.

Until now. This encounter could not yet be called a miss.

His bitter heart resisted anything even vaguely resembling prayer to any faith. Instead, his thoughts maintained a silent litany: *I'm not here. I'm not here. I'm not here.* Though there seemed little reason to cling to life, of one thing he was certain...no one would claim justice on him for the righteous vengeance he had wrought. Tran did not deserve to be mourned. He did not deserve to be remembered, save as a warning to others.

Barely realized at first, Paolo's breathing increased, growing louder and more aggressive as he thought of the man who had brutalized and killed his sister. The sound filled the small space where Paolo hid until he worried it would filter out to the storage compartment beyond.

He buried his rage before it betrayed him. Slowing his heartbeat and muffling his breath, he curled his body into a compact ball as only a trained contortionist could, head nestled in the pocket formed of arms and tucked knees. *I'm not here. I'm not here. I'm not here.* Weary beyond bearing, Paolo lost himself in sleep's oblivion as the phrase repeated in his head.

The subtle sound of engines cycling down to dock woke him.

Crap! He couldn't believe he'd overslept. Instinct ordered him to scramble for his post before Terlinda gave him more grief about penalty fees for missing their scheduled docking window. It was her favorite gripe. Swearing beneath his breath lest she hear him, Paolo jerked, snapping out of the knot he'd huddled in. Or tried to, anyway.

A nova erupted in his head as the back of his skull thudded against something hard, and his foot—likewise striking an unyielding surface—stung with the impact. Immediately, he curled back into a tight ball. *What the hell?* Where was he? Why wasn't he in his bunk? Drawing nearly spent air through clenched teeth, he resisted the urge to groan as he tried to fight past the pain. His lungs strained and more than sleep fogged his brain. It took him several long moments to realize what had happened. The reality he'd retreated from.

As he became more alert, Paolo examined the signs his subconscious had already interpreted. At some point during his ill-advised nap, the crates he'd hidden among had been loaded on a ship going God-knew-where.

"Mama dracului!" Paolo hissed the curse in his native Romani, *the devil's mother.*

Tears stung his eyes and he found himself close to his limit. Ready to give up...to embrace his fate. The Clans had a word: *Prikàza.* It meant retribution visited on one who upset the spiritual balance. In other words, the Devil's own luck. With each misfortune that befell him, Paolo found it harder to believe he was not such a one, though he could not believe Terlinda's *mulò* responsible, as legends claimed.

Locking his jaw, he banished thoughts of ill luck, lest they invite more, and with tight, controlled motions, maneuvered in his hiding space until he crouched by the end he had staged as his exit. Had the placement shifted during loading? Was he even now trapped with no room to move the loose container out of his way? He had to try as his cocoon of air swiftly soured, each breath ending in a low, harsh cough. Taking care not to press against any other surface but the one that should be safe, Paolo cautiously pushed outward. A faint scrape froze him.

Slower. He must not draw attention if any were around to hear. That bright and shiny thought set off another wave of worry. Sound or silence, it wouldn't matter if his exit opened in plain sight. Gritting his teeth, he forced the concern away, not ready to allow fear to literally suffocate him. Again he set his shoulder to the crate. Fraction of an inch by fraction of an inch, he edged it out from under the burden of its brothers. Even were he willing to shove his way out, it would not have been possible.

It took all of his strength just to shift the container in these careful measures.

And suddenly, even his strength was not enough.

Paolo clenched his eyes tight and swallowed his panic. He forced himself to run his hand slowly along the surface of the crate in search of any detail that might reveal the issue. As his fingers reached the bottom edge he had the answer. He'd pushed the obstacle far enough that it had tilted infinitesimally, wedging the crate between the pallet it rested on and the container above. Paolo settled back on his heels to consider the matter.

If he pressed upward enough to free the edge he could destabilize the tower of crates, bringing them down on top of him. Shoving with more force until the one stuck came free could cause the same fate. If he waited, surely he'd expend the last of the air before anyone would chance to find him (such would be a typical *Prikàza*). But...if he shifted his pressure...like so...and nudged down and out on the tilted edge...*like so*...

The crate landed with a soft thud onto what he presumed was a cargo bay floor. Paolo braced for what seemed inevitable, but the remaining stack did not, in fact, topple down on him. He drew several deep, shuddering breaths of fresher air into his lungs and grimly resisted the urge to drop prostrate in the space now sufficient to accommodate the length of him. He was not free of his unexpected prison yet, and even if he were, it courted danger to remain in the open. After resting a few moments he put his shoulder to the crate. Though both his lungs and his muscles burned, he once more pushed, this time in an effort to clear enough of a gap to crawl past the barrier. For a moment he feared himself trapped after all, but finally, with much straining, he created a gap just barely wide enough. Paolo silently thanked both his ancestors and carnival training equally as he contorted his muscles and turned his head, flattening sufficiently that he cleared the crates, losing no more than a layer or two of skin on either ear.

He slid his back along the top of the displaced crate and carefully drew out his legs until he moved free of the confinement. As he lay a moment in the near-dark, soundlessly catching his breath before he attempted to shove the crate back into place, he heard a noise; a hard thunk as of a hatch opening, followed by the sound of someone slowly clapping. An LED mega-cluster above his head came to instant life. Paolo tensed, his eyes squeezed closed against the sudden light. Spent, he wasn't quick enough to roll off of the crate. Before he could drop out of sight or reach, a firm grip pinned him in place.

"Consider me impressed," a man's gruff voice said from just above him. "For that matter, consider yourself impressed as well." A thick, calloused fist slammed into Paolo's jaw.

Paolo woke to jags of pain burning across various points of his body, but predominantly his jaw and his shoulders. The jaw was obvious. Being knocked senseless hadn't left him unable to remember how he'd gotten that way. But the shoulders...it took him a moment to figure that out. By the spread of his arms, it felt like someone had slid a roughly three-foot length of thick conduit across the base of his back and lashed his wrists around the ends, like a makeshift stock. Primitive, but damned effective.

There was little doubt, at this point, that the Fates had judged against him. Despair saturated his soul. He lay in the heap he'd been left in, head hanging, legs twisted, and back bowed. He didn't bother to look up at the sound of the hatch opening. In fact, he willed his body lax. Let them believe him still insensible. Nothing about his situation led him to expect this ship, or its crew were upstanding or legal. Better to use this moment to observe and perhaps learn something he could turn to his favor.

By the distinctly different footsteps, Paolo knew three people had entered the chamber. Three men, he would guess by the heavy sound of each tread. Two moved to either side of him. Before he realized their intent they had each gripped an end of his stock and hauled him up high until his feet dangled like a puppet's. And still, he forced his body to remain slack. The men just laughed and shook him until his arms screamed as he himself would not. Paolo resisted the urge to lash out with the legs they'd foolishly left unbound. He did send a silent command to the nanites beneath his skin to project the illusion of continued unconsciousness, though, before opening his eyes to study his captors.

Rough and prosperous were the first words he'd use to describe them. They appeared like standard space tramps, lean and hungry with banged-up gear, but each of them wore quality compression suits that gave lie to their overall impression. Their suits were void of any markings for rank or identification. Each of them had a utility pouch slung around their hips.

"Enough," the third man said with firm authority as he sauntered up to stand before them. He ran his hands over Paolo like a customer assessing goods in the market. "Bloody hell...a Gyp."

Paolo gritted his teeth at the racial slur but continued pretending unconsciousness.

The leader's hand locked on Paolo's chin, gripping it hard. He forced Paolo's head back until they stared eye to eye, though only Paolo was aware of that. He cataloged the man's face: square, with a cleft chin and too-full lips, hard eyes, and heavy brow. A thin, straight scar marred the left cheek, and another, more jagged example bisected his right eyebrow. His teeth were decent enough, but his breath foul. Paolo barely bothered noting the dark brown hair. It was too easily changed. But that face. Paolo would remember it. The Rom believed in vengeance nearly as much as luck, be it good or bad.

Oblivious to Paolo's true state, the leader went on. "No. Not worth keeping. Too big to crawl the conduits...too small to be of use for anything else that needs doing." Then the man tracked a finger over Paolo's tattooed face. "Besides, he's a Gypsy... definitely not worth the amount of trouble he'd be.

"We'll leave him with the rest of the marks," the leader continued. "Strip him of anything worth having and then get your asses back to the cargo bay. We have less than an hour to shift the goods over to the *Barbary* and disengage before this heap dives into the asteroid belt."

The man pivoted abruptly and headed for the hatch.

Something in his words triggered a memory. Faint, but insistent. Aside from the luxuries they offered, the Rom made great trade in information. A while back the Kalderaš Clan had learned of a band of pirates operating in fringe space, the areas past the edges of the more active trade routes. One of the known pirate vessels was the *Barbary*.

Paolo bared his teeth at the departing man's back, only to hiss in pain as his holders dropped him abruptly to the ground. Ingrained training had him remain relaxed as he fell. He didn't tense until the first booted foot took him beneath the ribs. Something cracked and he could not help but cry out. Pride cut the cry off and experience prompted Paolo to tense his muscles against the rest of the men's blows, but not to fight back. Understandably his illusion of unconsciousness fell away as his focus turned toward minimizing the beating. He did not let it go on for long, just enough to satisfy the thugs, before begging mercy. They laughed and aimed a few more kicks until their leader's voice sounded over the wall comm.

"Get your asses to the bay! Anything we're forced to leave behind comes out of your cut."

Paolo, struggling to breathe and startled by the sudden sound, lost focus on his tormentors. An unexpected kick connected forcefully with his already abused jaw. What color existed in the hold bled off leaving Paolo's vision briefly awash in shades of grey. He closed his eyes and fought not to be sick as his head bobbed uncontrollably. When rough hands began to paw among his clothing he attempted to kick out at them. The men laughed, the sound oddly muffled, as they slapped his feet away. He bucked and thrashed as they stripped him of the little he had left in the world, all but his clothes. But when one of them snatched the velvet pouch containing Terlinda's remains from around his neck Paolo raged and tried to ram him with the end of the conduit.

"Give her back! That's worth nothing to you!"

He knew he should have kept his mouth shut even as he spoke, but by then it was too late. With a smug sneer, the pirate slid the pouch over his bald head in a blatant taunt. Paolo imprinted the man's face on his memory and lunged at him, but the other man yanked him back. Again, they laughed and one of them landed a punch in his gut. A shove sent him backward to the deck where the impact of his weight against the length of conduit felt as if it all but crushed his forearms. Before they could start beating him again, the wall comm squawked once more. Paolo recognized the leader's voice, though he could not make out the words past the agony buzzing through his brain.

He lay in a haze as his assailants delivered parting blows, then left the chamber, harsh laughter trailing behind them.

It would be so easy to give in to his misery and fate, were it not so contrary to the Rom nature. Paolo instead focused on his pain. On compressing it. On shoving it deep into a mental hole where he could not feel it.

A lifetime of training returned his breath to slow, steady measures and his will forced each abused muscle to relax as he assessed his situation. Whatever the reason for his assailants' primitive measures, they worked to Paolo's favor. First, he tested the bonds around his wrists. He gritted his teeth as he flexed his hands and attempted to roll his wrists. It did not feel as though they'd bound him with rope or cord. It took effort, but he dropped his gaze and bent his body until he could just see the dull grey strips of duct tape that held him secure.

Paolo cursed. He did not have time to strip the tape, presuming there was even a surface to scrape it against. The leader had said they'd not quite an hour before the un-piloted craft entered the asteroid belt...and almost certain destruction.

About ten minutes had already passed. Paolo would have to work fast to free himself. Vengeance demanded it, as did the sheer cussedness of the Rom, which drove Paolo to preserve what life he had whether it seemed worth the living or not. At the end of everything, the Romani people were survivors. And even if Paolo were not confident of his own will to live, the leader of these rogues mentioned marks...victims. He would not stand by as more innocents like his sister were lost. The pirates were known for attacking colonizers, mostly automated ships sent out beyond settled space in search of inhabitable planets. That meant some-where on this vessel as many as 160 people were ensconced in preservation tanks. The cargo the pirates stripped from the ship were the colonists' settlement supplies and what little personal goods they had paid to bring along. In other words, goods that meant the world to them. The Rom themselves had a history of picking pockets or fleecing the unwary, but seldom of robbing marks of their livelihood or *lives*.

Anger sent tension through Paolo's body. Tension was counterproductive to the task at hand. Closing his eyes and emptying his thoughts, Paolo instead focused on the muscles in his shoulders, arms, back, abdomen, and buttocks. With fine adjustments he worked them, stretching and contorting respectively, until slowly his hips and ass rested on the conduit, then slid back over it. For a few moments, he allowed himself to rest, jaw clenched against the pain the familiar actions caused his abused flesh before he buried it deep once more. He sat with the conduit wedged beneath his thighs, arms stretched taut and head pounding. In his mind, he heard Terlinda's voice muttering and kvetching: *No...no... No stopping in the middle. There will be time for resting when you've ended the bastards.* Paolo could almost picture the outrage snapping in her dark, doe-like eyes and chuckled before he remembered. Outside of his thoughts, he would never hear her bossing him again. But she was right, figment or not. Those men had taken her from him all over again, stealing the last thing that mattered to Paolo, just as they threatened to do to the unsuspecting colonists.

He was not ashamed to admit that Terlinda mattered to him more, though he would gladly thwart the pirates in all the evil they planned. Taking his time in freeing himself would not get her back. With the memory of his sister driving him, Paolo manipulated his body, moving and contorting, stretching his back until there was room enough between himself and the conduit to allow his knees to pass. He then bent and tucked them against his chest and flattened his toes until they also pushed their way past the length of pipe, which along with his arms, now curled in front of him. For a brief instant, Paolo laid there trembling, breath sawing past lungs that would not fill fully as damaged ribs painfully reminded him of their presence. Even so, triumph sang the length of his nerves at this small success. But he was not yet free.

Fighting to ignore the muscle aches and pain pricks in his arms, Paolo drew them up toward his face, shifting his shoulders until his right wrist came within reach of his mouth. The skin was puffy and red and the fingers tingled. He tried not to think of the passing minutes as he gnawed at the tape, desperate to find or create an edge that he could then strip away. All the while his experienced ears strained for the subtle changes in the engine noises. Had the men fled to the other vessel yet? He did not believe so, as the ship's engine worked hard as if burdened beyond standard specifications.

He could not let the thought distract him from his task. Biting and tearing, biting and tearing. With a deep-felt urgency, he tore his way through the tape, stopping only to spit as the fragments clung to his tongue, leaving a chemical residue that caused his mouth to water in protest, which interfered with his efforts. Finally, the last strands snapped. He nearly screamed as every nerve ending flared and pulsed with restored blood flow.

"*Căcat!*" *Shit!* Paolo bit off the curse as he shook the hand to restore sensation enough to free his other wrist. He lost some skin in his haste as he ripped the last of the tape away. Weary and aching, he wanted nothing more than to sink to the deck and let his body recover, but time would not allow it. He had thirty minutes left to save his ass and the ship with it.

And all he could think of was getting his sister back.

Paolo scrambled to his feet and staggered to the hatch, his body throbbing with the wasted effort. No matter how he worked the bolt, the way remained barred. The pirates had locked the compartment, showing an annoying bit of foresight. Gritting his teeth, Paolo turned to the wall comm. A standard-issue unit, it had basic system access: emergency alerts, ship-wide communications, climate controls for the compartment, and a bare-bones ship's schematic, enough to show someone where they were and how to get around through the corridors. Not enough to show Paolo the maintenance infrastructure, but it did identify the ship's class, which served just as well. A nomadic race dependent on spacecraft for their existence, the Rom made sure all in the Clan had a basic knowledge of existing ship design; how to identify them, fly them, and—if need be—disable them. Paolo himself had excelled beyond basic in all three regards. He easily recognized the ship as a Portmann-class colonizer. The Portmanns were an economical design, compact and frugal with space. According to the schematic, he was not far from the engine room. If he could get there he could sabotage the engines before the ship nose-dived among the asteroids.

Paolo searched the walls for a maintenance hatch. He discovered it in the corner of the room and nearly broke his vow to never again lift a prayer to any god as he dropped to his knees, hands running frantically around the edge of the removable panel. A shuddering, relieved sigh sent sharp jags of pain through his abused torso as he found the pressure points that popped the panel away from the wall. Perhaps he wasn't quite as cursed as he feared... Paolo cut the thought off and made a sign against evil.

Such careless hope tempted the Fates to prove a man wrong.

He was about to duck through the hatch into the infrastructure of the ship when instinct drew his shoulders tight and made his belly burn. The memory of the strength and cruelty of his captors stopped him mid-crouch. Paolo turned and snatched up the conduit to which he'd been secured. It would make a serviceable club, if just a bit unwieldy.

At least nominally armed, he exited the compartment. He set the pipe down and pulled the hatch back into place behind him before picking up his makeshift weapon once more. Then he oriented himself, calling to mind the memory of the schematic and marrying it to his knowledge of the Portmann design. Paolo crouched and slipped in among the conduits and wires, contorting himself to pass through the infrastructure. He kept an eye to his left, watching for the reinforced bulkheads visible at regular intervals to mark the proper distance past the intervening compartments. When he judged he had gone far enough he turned left, and made his way through another tangle, before stopping by a full-sized maintenance hatch. If memory served, this brought him to a corridor that led to the engine room. Unfortunately, this was as far as the maintenance area extended. The heavily armored engine room was self-contained in case of catastrophic failure. From here he must venture into the open.

Not for the first time in his short life Paolo wished the holographic properties in his tattoos could be used to appear invisible. Such an illusion was beyond the capability of the nanites embedded beneath his skin, however. Instead, he used his skills as a sneak—something all among the Rom learned almost before they walked—to keep to the shadows created by the support struts that ran the length of the corridor at intervals.

Ten minutes had passed since he'd escaped when the corridor he traveled intersected with another. The sound of boots thudding on the deck came from his right. Paolo pressed himself into the shadow of the nearest strut. He stilled his breathing and visualized the nanites mimicking the wall behind him. Not the same as being invisible, but close, as long as he did not move. The footsteps came closer and Paolo could not completely silence the growl that rumbled in his throat as a familiar, bald-headed man entered the intersection. Terlinda's velvet pouch still hung around the pirate's neck.

Paolo struggled to remain motionless. Every nerve prickled with the need to snatch her away. His grip tightened on the length of conduit and he slowly eased his foot forward only to draw back as another voice called out from down the corridor at Paolo's back.

"Yo, Bock. What the hell are ya doin'? Cap's lookin' for ya. He's pissed."

Paolo squeezed his eyes closed and pressed tighter into his corner niche, his ears straining for any indication the man drew closer.

Bock stopped, casting an annoyed look over his shoulder. "Forgot somethin'. I'll be right there."

The slightest bit of tension eased from Paolo's shoulders. He could hear the footsteps fading as the other pirate walked away.

Bock grimaced. A hard light glimmered in his eye as he turned and continued the way he'd been heading. Paolo fought back the urge to cry out in frustration. The pirate moved in the opposite direction of the engine room. Paolo could follow the man. He could stalk in Bock's wake, waiting for a chance to reclaim the pouch containing his sister's remains, but would there still be time to stop the vessel from its ill-fated rendezvous with the asteroid belt?

Paolo sighed in frustration. His gut burned with the decision he knew had to be made. There were lives at stake and Terlinda would not have thanked him for putting the dead before the living. He couldn't go anywhere, however, until the way was clear. Creeping to the end of the corridor, he willed the nanites to mimic the floor, then dropped low to peer around the corner.

Bock had stopped in front of a compartment with *Cryo-Storage* stenciled beside the hatch. His manner and the way his gaze kept darting down the corridor spoke of the man's desire not to be caught. Paolo tensed as Bock opened the hatch and slid inside. Something in his expression echoed Paolo's memories of Tran.

Instinct sent Paolo to his feet and halfway to the cryo-storage compartment before the conscious decision had been made. As he walked he called to mind every detail of the pirate captain's face...his clothes...the timber of his voice. Every nasty expression and unconscious mannerism. With each step, Paolo transformed a little more until he stood before the compartment as the perfect image of the man who'd condemned him. He slowly opened the hatch to the sight of Bock running his fingers over the surface of a preservation tank he prepared to extract. If not for the trans-alum glass the man's hand would have fondled the young girl encased inside. Fury lunged up from Paolo's belly in reaction, drawing his muscles taut and rolling his lips back in a snarl. The girl looked nothing like his sister, but wore Terlinda's face all the same, in Paolo's mind. His breathing sped up and his fingers tightened on the conduit he still carried. He must have made a noise because Bock pivoted around. Judging from the way the man's face paled the nanites must have translated Paolo's rage onto the pirate captain's expression.

"Aw, come on, Cap...can't we bring along just one? We could all use a soft berth to sink anchor in..."

Paolo growled and fought the violent impulses bombarding him. In the back of his thoughts, a clock frantically ticked away the doomsday hour. There wasn't enough time to beat the bastard to a pulp. The desire must have translated to his expression, though.

Bock fell silent but did not move away from the preservation tank. He looked sullen, the set of his jaw rebellious as he shifted his stance into something more dangerous.

"She's mine, then," he insisted as he pivoted fully around, body tense and aggressive. "My cut of the spoils ...you can't argue against that, yeah?"

Paolo's gaze fixed on the pouch hung around the man's neck. His fingers ached to snatch it from the man's dead carcass. All it would take was a solid swing of the conduit to the side of Bock's bald head. It was an effort to resist, but Paolo had to if he and the unsuspecting colonists were to come out of this alive.

He focused on channeling the pirate captain. Voices were trickier than physical appearance, but Paolo was a fair mimic.

"Get back to the *Barbary*, now," he ordered in Cap's voice. "Or I'll kill you myself and you'll have no share! We're running out of time."

Bock's features hardened and his eyes took on a hard gleam that did not bode well for Paolo. The pirate started forward, his hands fisting, when the comm engaged and the captain's voice crackled across the line.

"Bock, you have two minutes to get your ass on the *Barbary* or we're leaving you behind. We've got a military cruiser headed this way."

The captain's words triggered a violent pounding in Paolo's chest. A military cruiser? What were the chances it was tracking him? He couldn't figure out how, but clearly, they had some way. Farfetched as it sounded, it began to look like his name had changed to *Prikàza*. On the bright and shiny side, his bad luck likely improved the colonists' and his own chances of survival. Of course, that last might have proved a bit too optimistic, judging from the way Bock looked at him.

The pirate's expression cycled from stunned to disbelieving and settled on enraged. As the man lunged forward, Paolo raised the length of conduit and swung it with all his might. The blow connected with Bock's shoulder and sent him careening into the bulkhead. The pirate caught himself and pushed back until he aimed at Paolo once more.

"I don't know how you did it, but you're dead, Gyp," Bock growled, making the only assumption he could.

Paolo laughed, his borrowed face set in grim lines. "I'm not that lucky," he said as he swung again, only to have the pirate grab the conduit. Before he could remove it from Paolo's grasp the ship jerked beneath their feet, likely jarred by the *Barbary's* ion wake as the pirate ship departed with haste. Or maybe they'd already entered the edges of the asteroid belt. Either way, the disruption sent both combatants to the deck in a heap, Paolo on top, smiling with satisfaction.

If there was anything the Rom knew it was how to fight dirty.

As the two of them tumbled, Paolo released his grip on the conduit and instead grabbed for the pouch hanging around

Bock's neck. He then yanked the man's head toward him as he sent his own slamming forward. Blood erupted from Bock's nose and his eyes rolled into his head. Paolo got his feet beneath him and fought the urge to twist the lanyard in his hands until Bock's face went blue. Breathing hard with the effort to resist, Paolo instead spat on the pirate.

"Well you're certainly not good enough for *my* sister!" he growled as he slipped Terlinda's remains over the unconscious man's head, before kicking him back to the deck. Paolo hung the pouch once more around his own neck and quickly secured Bock with duct tape from the pirate's utility pouch.

Biting back a groan of pain from his earlier beating, Paolo struggled to control his breathing. He lost himself a moment as his eyes locked on the young girl in her preservation tank. So like his sister…and yet so not like her. Something healed within his heart at knowing he had kept this one safe.

The jarring, raucous sound of a proximity alarm broke Paolo from his musing. He lunged for the wall comm by the compartment hatch and called up the ship's alert system. He cursed at what he saw.

There wasn't time to stop the vessel from entering the asteroid belt. Fortunately, the Portmann class had decent hull shielding—more than capable of absorbing blows from the dust, pebbles, and head-sized rocks that mostly made up an asteroid belt—and it was equipped with auto cannons that could take care of the bigger bits, as long as someone was at the helm to steer around anything the size of a shuttlecraft or larger. Paolo swallowed hard as acid scored his throat. Their only hope now lay in *him* navigating a path through that relentlessly tumbling obstacle course. He was better than good as a pilot, but navigating an asteroid belt alone was a tricky proposition.

As he ran for the command deck, Paolo gripped Terlinda's remains and prayed for all he was worth.

Glossary

A chuisle mo chroí!: Irish Gaelic, a term of endearment meaning "o pulse of my heart."

Áes Sidhe: The people of the hills. It was one of the names given to the old Irish gods, the Tuatha de Danaan, when they retreated under the hills (*Sidhe*) after their defeat by the Milesians.

A ghrá!: Irish Gaelic for "O love!"

Anu: In Celtic lore, an alternate name for the goddess Danu, from whom the Tuatha de Danaan took their name. The names are used interchangeably throughout the mythology, though there is some debate as to whether these were one and the same goddess, or two separate ones. In the author's fabricated legend of Danu's time before arriving in Ireland Anu is not a variant on the name Danu but a person in her own right, Danu's older twin. For the purpose of this fiction, Anu sacrifices herself to allow Danu to escape the clutches of the Namhaid, the enemy. In reverence Danu uses both names after the crossing to Ireland, ensuring that her beloved sister will ever be remembered (thus explaining the presence of both names in the actual Celtic mythology and Irish place names). In the author's created mythology to allow her sister to escape the Namhaid, Anu uses magic and her own soul to create the lesser fae creatures of the world. Because of this, her soul was not lost when she was taken by the Namhaid, but it also could not return to the Daoine Maithé after her death because only her body died. As the faelings died, parts of her soul gathered and were ultimately channeled into a human birth through Danu's intervention in an effort to preserve the babe, which would have been lost, and to bring Anu back into the world. The child born, Kara O'Keefe, is a melding of both human and *Sidhe*, but without the drawbacks of being a Halfling. Through Anu's soul, she is linked to the faelings and the portion of the soul they still possess.

Ard Namhaid: a combination of the Irish Gaelic words for High (Ard) and enemy (Namhaid). These are a fictitious caste of a race created by the author to explain several key points in the Celtic myth of which no details are known. The Ard are all male and dominate the Namhaid. In appearance, they are similar to the Namhaid Conairt (the female of the species), with a fine, velvety white pelt and dagger-like teeth in a blood-red mouth, however, their hair and eyes are deepest black, whereas the females' hair and eyes are red. Also, though their hands are likewise clawed, they are nowhere as pronounced as those of the Namhaid Conairt. (*See also* Bás; Namhaid Conairt.)

Ard Ri: Irish Gaelic for "High King."

Bás: Irish Gaelic for Death. In the author's created mythology, this is the name the Namhaid, the ancient enemy race of the *Sidhe*, have for themselves. In *Tomorrow's Memories,* they are given the name Namhaid na Tuatha by Goibhniu, which translates to Enemy of the People.

Beag Scath: A combination of the Irish Gaelic words meaning Little (beag) and Shadow (scath). The name Maggie gave the sprite that became emotionally attached to her long ago in Eire. The sprite eventually bonds with Kara and follows her everywhere.

Bean Fianna: For the purpose of this story, the women warriors of the *Sidhe Fianna.*

Bean Sidhe: translating into "a woman of the hills," the Bean *Sidhe,* or banshee, is a faerie harbinger of death. Appearing as a woman in a green dress and grey cloak, with eyes fiery red from weeping, she is seen scrubbing bloody garments in a stream or heard wailing outside a household where a family member is doomed to die. If the bean *Sidhe* is caught, she must relinquish the name of the doomed. When multiple bean *Sidhe* wail together they are heralding the death of a great or holy person. Cliodna, the goddess of beauty, is bean *Sidhe* to the Clan O'Keefe.

Beyond the Veil: a Celtic euphemism for dying.

Bodhran: Pronounced *bow-rawn*, a Celtic frame drum made of cured goat skin stretched taut over a wooden frame, played either by the tapping of the fingers or with a double-headed stick called a cipín, tipper, or beater.

Bodega: A Spanish word meaning "store" or "grocery store." The term is commonly used in the ethnic neighborhoods of New York, where Kara and Tony are from.

Brian Boru: (960-1014) The last High King, or Ard Ri, of Ireland. He defended Ireland against the attacks of the Vikings and ended that race's hopes of ever taking the island.

Brownie: In Scottish Celtic Mythology a domestic fairy known for doing nightly deeds for those who treat them kindly. Their coloring is representative of their name. They are commonly left offerings of milk in thanks.

By the silver hand o' Nuada!: A curse fabricated by the author and used by Maggie in *Yesterday's Dreams*. It is a reference to Nuada of the Silver Hand, the first ruler of the de Danaan, who lost his hand in a battle with the Firbolg (one of the many groups that inhabited Ireland before the de Danaan arrived). The injury cost him his rule because no king could rule who was not whole and able to defend his people. He was presented with his silver hand by Dian Cécht, the god of medicine, but it was not enough for him to take up his kingship. Later, Dian Cécht's son, Miach, made him a hand of flesh and blood and Nuada once again ruled the de Danaan. The basic implication of the curse is "our greatest efforts sometimes fail at great cost."

Căcat!: Romani for "Shit!"

Camlo: Romani for "lovely one."

Carmán: An Athenian goddess (possibly rooted in the Greek goddess Demeter) who, with her three sons: Calma (Valiant), Dubh (Black), and Olcas (Evil), terrorized early Ireland. They were eventually defeated by the Tuatha de Danaan. She was bound in chains and her three sons destroyed. It is said Carmán died of grief. Carmán is also portrayed as a goddess of black magick, destroying anything by chanting a spell three times. (There are several different accountings of the names of the goddess's sons, but for the purpose of this series the author has chosen to adhere to those names listed in the first accounting of this legend that was encountered during the research phase.)

Chey: Romani for "girl".

Cimbalom: a concert hammered dulcimer typically found in Hungary and the central-eastern countries that made up Austria-Hungary in the late 19th, early 20th centuries. A type of chordophone composed of a large, trapezoidal box with metal strings stretched across its top. It is (typically) played by striking two beaters against the strings. The steel treble strings are arranged in groups of 4 and are tuned in unison. The bass strings which are over-spun with copper, are arranged in groups of 3 and are also tuned in unison.

The Cosaint: Irish Gaelic for safeguard. A legend of the author's creation developed to support her extrapolation of why the *Sidhe* are called Tuatha de Danaan (The Children of Danu). The Cosaint is a *Sidhe* woman hidden at birth so that not even she knows what she is. Raised as a human, she is meant to be a safeguard against the *Sidhe* race being destroyed without a means of the souls returning to the earth, as nearly happened in the author's fabricated tale when Danu herself was the last of her kind and had to hide from the Namhaid.

Cúchulainn (the Hound of Culann): One of the most famous heroes in Irish mythology. Originally called Sétanta, Cúchulainn got his name from defending himself and slaying the hound that defended the fortress of Culann, after which he vowed to defend the fortress himself until a new hound could be found and trained, thus becoming known as the Hound of Culann. Though his achievements are many, he is chiefly known for his single-handed defense of Ulster during the war of the Táin.

Curragh of Kildare: The place where Earl Gerald is said to ride his horse around every seven years. To this day the region is known for the horse racing that takes place there.

Danu: In Irish Celtic mythology, the goddess from whom the Tuatha de Danaan took their name; for the purpose of this story, the birth mother of every *Sidhe* born in Ireland. The sole survivor of a concerted attack on the *Sidhe* in their original homelands, she alone remained to give birth to the *Sidhe* souls returning for their next incarnation. Though Kara is unaware, she was born when Danu joined with Kara's mother, making Kara born of the goddess Danu as well, which is how she came to possess a *Sidhe* soul.

Daoine Maithé: Irish Gaelic for "Good People", one of the names by which the *Sidhe* are called. In the author's created mythology, this is also the name by which the *Sidhe* originally called themselves, before coming to Ireland and becoming the *Tuatha de Danaan.*

Dearmad: Irish Gaelic for "forget."

Dinlo: Romani for "stupid," "fool," or "idiot."

Eire: The original name for Ireland.

Elf-kin: the author's term for those of mixed *Sidhe* and human parentage, the non-derogatory term for waterkin.

Falias, Finias, Gorias, and Murias: Four great cities said to be the former home of the Tuatha de Danaan before they arrived in Ireland. Nothing more specific is mentioned of their original homeland. Each city contained a magical artifact that the Tuatha de Danaan carried with them to Ireland.

Faelings: a term encompassing the "lesser" fae of mythology. In the author's usage, it represents the more wild, natural fae such as the pixies, sprites, etc. Also called by the author the kin-cousins to denote that they are related to the *Sidhe*, but not of them. These are Anu's Children, created and sent out in the world to muddy the trail so that Danu could escape from the Namhaid.

Fear Fianna: For the purpose of this story, the men warriors of the *Sidhe Fianna.*

The Fe-Fiada: In Irish Celtic mythology, a supernatural mist or fog.

Fianna: In Ireland's far past these were the warriors who were the royal bodyguard for the Ard Ri, the High King. (*See also, Sidhe* Fianna)

Fionn Mac Cumhail (Finn Mac Cool): One of the most celebrated heroes in Irish myth. Born Demna, he gained the name of Fionn (the Fair One) when he burnt his finger on the flesh of the Salmon of Knowledge, which he was cooking for his master. Sucking his thumb to cool it, he obtained wisdom from the magical fish. He went on to become the leader of the *Fianna,* the royal bodyguard. His wife was the goddess Sadb, who was originally transformed into a fawn by a spurned Druid, who eventually whisks away and transforms her back into a fawn again while she is pregnant with Fionn's son. Fionn never found his wife, but his son, whom he named Oisín (fawn), eventually was discovered and came to be with him.

Fledh Ghoibhnenn: The Otherworld feast held by the Smithgod Goibhniu. Any mortal to take part in the feast and the drink served becomes immortal.

Gadje: Romani for "outsider." (Also see Gorgio.)

Garda Faoi Rún: A combination of the Irish Gaelic words Garda (guard) and Faoi Rún (in secret). The name given to the sprite answering to Aí, left with Agnieszka to look over her until she could be brought to safety. Also called Rex by Agnieszka.

Geal leanbh: Irish Gaelic for "cherished child."

Geal leannán: Irish Gaelic for "cherished lover."

Gearoidh Iarla (Earl Gerard): A great man of the Fitzgeralds, he had a rath (fortress) at Mullaghmast. He was known for standing against injustice and for his abilities to transform himself into any form. It is said that he and his warriors now sleep in a long cavern under the Rath of Mullaghmast. Every seven years the Earl rides around the Curragh of Kildare on a white steed with silver-shod hooves. At a time when those hooves are worn thin as a cat's ear, the miller's son with six fingers to each hand will blow his trumpet to wake the warriors and Gearoidh Iarla will return to the land of the living. He will defend Ireland against their enemies, and reign as Ireland's king for two-score years, or seventy times seven, depending on the account.

The Gentry: One of the names given to the *Sidhe* by the common folk so that they could be referred to without invoking their name or drawing their uncomfortable attention.

Glamory: A spell to make whatever the caster wishes—himself, an object, or another person—appear other than it really is.

Goibhniu the Smith: An Irish/Celtic blacksmith god. Son of the goddess Danu. He manufactures swords that always strike true, and he possesses the mead (ale) of eternal life. He is also considered the god of healing due to the role of iron in Celtic life and the magical properties it is said to have. Goibhniu presides over an Otherworld feast (Fledh Ghoibhnenn) where any mortal to take part becomes immortal; exempt from common death and disease. In some accounts, this is attributed to the food, and in most others, it is attributed to the ale or mead given to drink at the Feast.

Gorgio: In England, the term the Romani use for non-Gypsy folk, "outsider."

Grimoires: ancient, mystical texts, usually full of dark occult knowledge. These texts contain the spells and references that represent painstaking research and experimentation, often of the dark arts, though the term has come to imply any book of spells, be they Black or White magic.

Hounds (Celtic): well respected by royalty and warriors. Symbols of honor. The name was assumed as a title of loyalty and courage. They were the traditional guardians of roads and crossroads, protecting and guiding lost souls to the Otherworld.

For the purpose of this story, a reference to Aí, Goibhniu's messenger and Hound. He is sent to safeguard the Cosaints in *Tomorrow's Memories*, and to rescue the souls of the Namhaid's victims in *Today's Promise*. He is not the only one sent out on these tasks.

Imeacht gan teacht ort: An Irish Gaelic curse meaning "may you leave without returning".

Kushti: Romani for "good, fine, nice, all right."

Lavuta: Romani for violin.

Leanbh: Irish Gaelic for "child."

Leprechaun: In Irish Celtic Mythology a diminutive member of the fairy folk known for making shoes, but only one at a time, never in pairs.

Lhiannon: Irish Gaelic for "Sweetheart."

Mallacht mo chait ort: Irish Gaelic for "My cat's curse upon you."

Mama dracului!: Romani curse meaning "the devil's mother."

Mamó: Irish Gaelic for "Grandma."

Manannan Mac Lir: Ruler of Tír Tairnigiri (the Land of Promise). A shape-changer, he is depicted with a mantle and helmet of invisibility (or flames) and an unfailing sword. He was also attributed with bring fertility and prosperity and was associated with the cauldron of regeneration.

Mar aon ó thús, mar aon go deo: Irish Gaelic an idiom meaning "As one from the beginning, as one forever." (A big thank you to Mary Kinsella for this phrasing and translation.)

Marime: Romani for "dirty, unclean."

Mathair: Irish Gaelic for "Mother."

The Miller's Son: It is said in the legend of Gearoidh Iarla, that the miller's son, who will be born with six fingers on each hand, will blow his trumpet and wake those who sleep beneath the Rath of Mullaghmast.

Mizhak: Romani for 'Wicked.'

Namhaid: Irish Gaelic for "enemy." A fictitious race created by the author, they are the reason why the people who would come to be known as the *Sidhe* flee their original homes in Falias, Finias, Gorias, and Murias. The Enemy slays all but one of the *Sidhe*, a young elf named Danu. She escapes and flees to Ireland, there to bear her children, who from that day forward are known by the name Tuatha de Danaan, or the Children (People) of Danu. In *Tomorrow's Memories* Goibhniu calls them by the name *Namhaid na Tuatha*, which translates to Enemy of the People. Their own name for themselves is *Bás,* (Irish Gaelic for "Death").

The Namhaid Conairt: a combination of the Irish Gaelic words for "enemy" (Namhaid) and "pack" (Conairt). As created by the author, these are the hunter caste of the *Namhaid* (or the *Bás,* as they call themselves) responsible for hunting down the elves and either capturing or killing them. They are all female, with a fine, velvety white pelt and flowing deep, red hair. Their eyes are likewise red, and their teeth like dainty daggers in their blood-red mouths. Each hand is clawed with dagger-like nails, while those on the feet are blunted from running and capable of gouging, not slicing. The Conairt do not eat when they are breeding and they do not bear their own young. When they mate the sperm and eggs are stored in a sack at the base of the spine. Once a suitable host is found, the eggs are extruded through a barb that extends like a retractable tail from the female. Jabbed into the body of the victim, the eggs are seated in the abdomen. The individual so implanted is for all intents and purposes dead as a chemical injected with the sack inhibits the thought centers of the brain, allowing only the autonomous impulses to operate, and those only barely.

The Naming: In the author's created mythology, this is a ceremony where the *Sidhe* chose their public name, the one they will be known by in the world, reserving their given name for use among the *Tuatha de Danaan.* In Today's Promise, Kara takes part in the Naming, but because her given name is already the name she is known by in the world, she chooses her private name for use among the *Sidhe.* There is an uproar when she chooses the name 'Anu', which was the name bore by the twin of the goddess Danu, the only *Sidhe* never to be reborn. At the end of the ceremony, Kara reveals that she *is* Anu reborn, a claim proven true when Anu's knotwork on the Great Wall fades away and a new one representing Kara appears at the end of the spiral.

Olcas: Irish Gaelic for "evil." This is also the name of one of the three sons of the Athenian goddess Carmán.

Pharo! Pharo!: An ancient Celtic battle cry, possibly a corruption of faire ó! ("Look out, ó!")

Pixie: In Irish Celtic Mythology a cheerful and mischievous fairy that adores music and dancing.

Prikàza: Romani for bad luck or bad omen.

Pucá (Pooka): in Irish Celtic mythology, a fey creature that leads travelers astray and performed other mischievous deeds. By some accounts it appears in the likeness of a fierce black steed that will pull the unwary onto his back run away with them through river and fen, not shaking them off until the grey of dawn.

Puridaia: Romani for grandmother.

Rakli: Romani for "non-Romani girl."

Rath: A fortress or earthwork, usually circular, surrounding a chieftain's house. This has also come to mean the hills where the Tuatha de Danaan retreated beneath after their defeat by the Milesians.

Rath o' Mullaghmast: The hill beneath which Gearoidh Iarla (Earl Gerald) is said to sleep. This is where legend says the miller's son will blow his trumpet.

Redcap: in Irish Celtic mythology, a fairy known by his red hat and bloodthirsty ways.

The Rom, The Romani: These are the nomadic gypsies most common in Europe but found in one form or another all around the world. They are known occasionally to settle, though they do not lose their gypsy ways.

Rom/Romni: A married man/woman of the Romani.

Romaniya: Romani laws and traditions, the Romani legal code

Selkie: In Irish Celtic mythology a creature of seal-like appearance that, when it sheds its pelt, assumes the likeness of a human. It is said that if anyone captures the shed pelt and hides it away, the selkie will remain with them forever as their mate, but should the selkie find the hidden skin it will return once more to the sea.

The Sidhe: Pronounced "shee," the Fair Folk, Otherworldly beings that came to live in Ireland in the time before it was invaded by the Milesians. After their defeat they were banished underground, living in mounds, also called *Sidhe*. They were said to be very long-lived, if not immortal, and possessing of mystical powers. (*See also,* Áes *Sidhe*, Daoine Maithé, The Gentry, Tuatha de Danaan)

The Sidhe Fianna: The author's created mythology for the purpose of this book. First seen in Tomorrow's Memories, a group of warriors selected by Goibhniu the Smithgod to combat the assaults being perpetrated against the *Sidhe* in this series. There are two groups of the *Sidhe Fianna*: the *Bean Fianna*, or warrior women, and the *Fear Fianna*, the warrior men.

Sowlth/Somhlth: In Irish Celtic mythology, a supernatural being without shape. Refers—for this series only—to Carmán's sons, who, for the author's purposes, were not destroyed but merely disembodied.

Sprite: Spirit faerie. Very creative, sprites are often depicted as muses, artists, and poets. They are some of the most creative fairies and may even decide to bond with a human or *Sidhe* and stay with them their whole lives.

Tír na mBan: The Land of Women or the Land of the Maidens. Part of the Irish Celtic Otherworld, the land ruled by Balor of the Fomorian giants.

Tír na nÓg: The Land of Youth. Part of the Irish Celtic Otherworld, this is where Goibhniu presides over the *Fledh Ghoibhnenn*.

Tír Tairnigiri: The Land of Promise. Part of the Irish Celtic Other-world, this is where Manannan Mac Lir, the major sea-god, held his seat of power.

Tuatha de Danaan: The Children of Danu, also translated in other texts as the People of Danu, another name for the *Sidhe*, said to be blessed by the goddess Danu, also called Anu or Danaa. The alternate, more common spelling is *Tuatha de Danann*, but as the version used was the first one the author encountered in her research, that is the one that appears in this series.

The Unraveling: In the author's created mythology this is a ritual by which the *Sidhe* banish one of their own for crimes too heinous to ignore. To all effects, they never existed and their soul, should they die, will never be reborn as a member of the *Sidhe* race. The banished one's soul is literally cut away from the racial collective. This collective has a visual representation in the form of a massive, interlocking knotwork design on the Great Wall, located in Goibhniu's Court in *Tír na nÓg*. By means of a ritual dagger, each living *Sidhe* must trace the knotwork pattern representing the banished one's life. When all have done so the soul's connection is severed. This also means the individual will no longer be able to enter the *Sidhe* Lands.

Vardo: a traditional Romani wagon meant for living in.

Waterkin: a term originating with the author to describe those of mixed blood, with both a *Sidhe* and human parent. It is originally a condescending term referring to the fact that the *Sidhe* blood has been diluted...watered down, thus less than the original, though repeated use has reduced it to merely an identifier. The more friendly term is elf-kin.

The Welcoming: In the author's created mythology, this is a ritual that is performed when one of the Tuatha de Danaan are pregnant. The *Sidhe* have a finite number of souls. Those souls are reborn as their decedents (this is extrapolated from elements of actual Celtic beliefs on reincarnation). Before a child is born the soul must first strip away the memories of the former life. By means of the ritual, the *Sidhe* who knew the individual who has passed help the soul shed its memories. All gather in a special glade. Those pregnant with the returning souls gather at the center of the glade and magical mists form a column around them. As they share the memories they have of the deceased, which appear on the column, the watching crowd shares theirs as well and the memory is released by the soul. While a soul will be reborn without this assistance, the time it takes would be longer without this mass purging.

Sources

Print Resources:
·Ellis, Peter Berresford, *A Dictionary of Irish Mythology.* (Santa Barbara, CA: ABC-CLIO, Inc, 1987.)
·*Ireland: The Complete Guide and Road Atlas*, 7th ed. (Guilford, CT: The Globe Pequot Press, 2002.)
·Mac Mathúna, Séamus and Ailbhe Ó Curráin, *Collins Gem: Irish Dictionary.* (New York: HarperCollins Publishers, 1995).
·Rolleston, T. W., *Celtic Myths and Legends.* (Mineola, NY: Dover, 1990.)
·Tong, Diane, *Gypsy Folk Tales.* (New York: MJF Books, 1989.)
·Yeats, W. B., *Irish Fairy & Folk Tales.* (New York: Barnes & Noble Books, 1993.)

Internet Resources:
Celtic Myth
·http://www.alia.ie/tirnanog/myth1.html
·http://www.livingmyths.com/Celticmyth.htm
·http://www.celticattic.com/olde_world/myths/fairy.htm
·http://www.ladywoods.org/roots4.htm
·http://www.seanachaidh.com/godcelt.html
·http://magickwell.20m.com/danu.htm
·http://www.danann.org/library/herb/cup2.html

·http://joellessacredgrove.com/Celtic/deitiesg-h-i.html
·http://www.deoxy.org/h_mounds.htm

Gypsies
·http://www.romani.org/
·http://www.christusrex.org/www2/gypsies.net/
·http://www.herts.ac.uk/UHPress/Gypsies.html

Miscellaneous
http://www.peevish.co.uk/slang/search.htm

About the Author

Award-winning author and editor Danielle Ackley-McPhail has worked both sides of the publishing industry for longer than she cares to admit. In 2014 she joined forces with husband Mike McPhail and friend Greg Schauer to form her own publishing house, eSpec Books.

Her published works include six novels, *Yesterday's Dreams, Tomorrow's Memories, Today's Promise, The Halfling's Court, The Redcaps' Queen,* and *Baba Ali and the Clockwork Djinn,* written with Day Al-Mohamed. She is also the author of the solo collections *A Legacy of Stars, Consigned to the Sea, Flash in the Can,* and *Transcendence,* the non-fiction writers' guide, *The Literary Handyman,* and is the senior editor of the *Bad-Ass Faeries* anthology series, *Gaslight & Grimm, Dragon's Lure,* and *In an Iron Cage.* Her short stories are included in numerous other anthologies and collections.

She is a member of Broad Universe, a writer's organization focusing on promoting the works of women authors in the speculative genres.

Danielle lives in New Jersey with husband and fellow writer, Mike McPhail, and three extremely spoiled cats.

To learn more about her work, visit www.sidhenadaire.com or www.especbooks.com.

Eternally Faithful Backers

Anonymous (2)
Adriane Ruzak
Alan Danziger
Amanda Johnson
Amelia Smith
Andreas Gustafsson
Arne Radtke
Ashley O.
Ashli T.
Barbara Silcox
Bodge, Elizabeth Inglee-
   Richards
Brenda Cooper
Bryan Young
Buzzy Multimedia
Carol J. Guess
Cat Rambo
Catherine Asaro
Catherine Gross-Colten
Charis
Charlie Tibbert
Craig Wright
Daniel Hiestand
David Goldstein
David McCready
DC Wilson

Donald J. Bingle
Donna H
Don't list
D-Rock
Ellen Montgomery
Emily Henshaw
Evaristo Ramos, Jr.
Frederick Doot
Gail Z. Martin
Gary Vandegrift
Gil Cnaan
Grace Tin Lo
Hal Greenberg
Jacalyn Boggs
James Chambers
James, Mostly Harmless
Jason Russell
Jean Marie Ward
Jean Rabe
Jeffrey Ponce
John C Barstow
John Green
John Idlor
Jon Quigley
Kacey Ezell
Katrina Goodwin

Keith Hall
Kelli Neier
Kelly Pierce
Kristen
Kristin Evenson Hirst
Larry "Lordlnyc" Nelson
Leona R, Wisoker
Linda Pierce
Louise Löwenspets
Marc D. Long
Margaret St. John
Mark Knapp Jr
Mary Spila
Melissa Hayden
Meriah Lysistrata Crawford
Missy Katano
Nanci Moy & David Bean
Nellie
Patrick Thomas
Patti Kinlock

Paul Bulmer
Pepita Hogg-Sonnenberg
Richard Groller
Rob Steinberger
Robert Helmbrecht
Robert Martincic
Rodney Romasanta
Sally Novak Janin
SAMK
Sharlene Glennie
Silence in the Library
    Publishing
Stephen Rider
Steve Lord
Susan Simko
SwordFire
T.Rob
Tom Carpenter
Vicki Hsu
William Fr